The bearer of this scroll, namely,

_____

is a wizard of the Shianti

THE WORLD of LONE WOLF
PAGE AND DEVER

The Author

IAN PAGE was born in London in 1960. Since the age of sixteen he has pursued a successful career as a singer/songwriter. With the band *Secret Affair*, he had a string of chart hits to his credit including 'Time for Action' and 'My World'. His interest in the fantastic worlds of 'Sword and Sorcery' dates back to his early teens, and to his love of the novels of J. R. Tolkien and Michael Moorcock. It was in 1979, when Joe Dever introduced him to role-playing games, that his involvement in the world of Magnamund began. He has since contributed greatly to the development of the southern reaches of this fantastic world, and has worked closely with Joe on several other role-playing games projects that include TV and radio appearances.

The Editor

JOE DEVER was born in 1956 at Woodford Bridge in Essex. His involvement with role-playing games dates back to 1977 when, on a trip to Los Angeles, he discovered 'Dungeons and Dragons'. In 1982 he won the Advanced Dungeons and Dragons Championships in America, where he was the only British competitor. His bestselling Lone Wolf adventures are the culmination of many years of developing the world of Magnamund. Printed in several languages and sold throughout the world, they have earned both him and illustrator Gary Chalk recognition as masters of the gamebook craft. Joe Dever also writes for modelling journals, is a contributing editor to *White Dwarf* — Britain's leading role-playing games magazine, adapts the Lone Wolf adventures for computer play and is noted for his model photography. Together with Gary Chalk, he produces the Lone Wolf Club Newsletter and enjoys answering letters from readers all over the world.

THE WORLD OF LONE WOLF

BOOK 1

Grey Star the Wizard

Written by Ian Page
Edited by Joe Dever
Illustrated by Paul Bonner

 BOOKS FOR YOUNG ADULTS

BERKLEY BOOKS, NEW YORK

This Berkley/Pacer Book contains the complete
text of the original edition.

GREY STAR THE WIZARD

A Berkley/Pacer book, published by arrangement with
Century Hutchinson Limited

PRINTING HISTORY
Beaver Books edition published 1985
Berkley/Pacer edition / February 1987

ISBN: 0-425-09590-8

Pacer is a trademark belonging to
The Putnam Publishing Group.

A BERKLEY BOOK ® TM 757,375
Berkley Books are published by The Berkley Publishing Group,
200 Madison Avenue, New York, New York 10016.
The name "BERKLEY" and the "B" logo
are trademarks belonging to Berkley Publishing Corporation.

PRINTED IN THE UNITED STATES OF AMERICA

20   19   18   17   16   15   14   13   12   11   10

To Joe Dever,
without whom . . .

ACTION CHART

MAGICAL POWERS

1	
2	
3	
4	
5	

BACKPACK

1	
2	
3	
4	
5	
6	
7	
8	

Can be discarded when not in combat

HERB POUCH (Maximum 6 articles)

1	
2	
3	
4	
5	
6	

Only carried if you possess
Magical Power of Alchemy

MEALS

(Carried in Backpack)
− 3 EP if no Meals available
when instructed to eat

BELT POUCH
containing Nobles (50 maximum)

COMBAT SKILL	WILLPOWER	ENDURANCE POINTS
	May go above Initial Score	Can never go above Initial Score 0 = dead

COMBAT RECORD

ENDURANCE POINTS	WILLPOWER POINTS		ENDURANCE POINTS
GREY STAR		COMBAT RATIO	ENEMY
GREY STAR		COMBAT RATIO	ENEMY
GREY STAR		COMBAT RATIO	ENEMY
GREY STAR		COMBAT RATIO	ENEMY
GREY STAR		COMBAT RATIO	ENEMY
GREY STAR		COMBAT RATIO	ENEMY

SPECIAL ITEMS
AND WEAPONS LIST

DESCRIPTION	KNOWN EFFECTS

WEAPONS (maximum 2 Weapons, Wizard's Staff counts as 1 Weapon)

1

2

If combat entered without Wizard's Staff −6 CS.
If combat entered without a Weapon −8 CS.

CS = Combat Skill   EP = Endurance

OF THE COMING OF GREY STAR

Ancient days they were when first the Shianti set foot upon the land that men call Magnamund. Long had they journeyed through the void, homeless wanderers in search of a place to call their own. And so it was that when the Shianti first looked upon the face of the land, their hearts were raised in wonder. They saw a world of nameless mountains, untamed forests and lands both wild and free. Here they chose to cease their wanderings and to devote themselves to the study and appreciation of this new found land.

To the delight of the Shianti, the race of man first emerged at this time and they watched his early struggle towards civilization with eager concern. Like gods, the Shianti seemed to the minds of primitive men. Tall and proud, shining with a radiance that spoke of magic and arcane mystery, the Shianti moved among them and with their powers of wizardry, aided man in his development.

As the centuries passed, man fell to worship of the magical Shianti and the power of these wizards grew even stronger. With hungry hearts they sought to unlock the mysteries of knowledge, sending their minds into other planes of existence and strange worlds beyond the sphere of the material plane. Their foresight was now unmatched and the power of their thought was mighty indeed. It was at this time that they created the Moonstone. Woven of the very fabric of the astral plane of Daziarn, this translucent gem was the greatest achievement of Shianti wisdom. It was the binding force of all Shianti magic, containing the combined might of all their wizardry, the sum of all their knowledge. The Golden Age of the Shianti had come and the Moonstone was the instrument of their dominion throughout all Magnamund. Man stood as little more than a shadow, blinded by the shining white light of Shianti glory. But, in creating the Moonstone, the unwritten laws of nature had been transgressed. For the Moonstone, like the Shianti themselves, was something outside of man's own world; it defied the natural order laid down by the creators of the Earth and disrupted the balance that the gods had designed.

The Goddess Ishir, High Priestess of the Moon and mother of all men, showed herself to the Shianti and spoke to them of the destiny of man: 'The children of this world must claim their inheritance. Their time has come and they must learn to stand alone. They are lost in their worship of you and the day draws ever nearer when they will covet the power of the Moonstone.'

And the Shianti said: 'Forgive us Great Goddess, for we intended no harm. We love mankind even as you do. We have sought to do good and protect your children from harm.'

But Ishir replied, 'Of this there can be no doubt, but this world is not your realm. Man must be free to pursue his destiny alone, and you must leave, for you trespass on his domain.'

10

The Shianti were filled with sorrow. They feared a return to the void and to their lonely wandering, and pleaded with Ishir that she might allow them to remain. Ishir was filled with pity for them. She spoke again, saying, 'If you are to remain you must obey my command. You must take a vow never to interfere with mankind's fate. As a token of good faith you must lay aside the Moonstone, and return it to the plane where it belongs.'

Solemnly, the Shianti agreed. The vow was sworn before Ishir, and the Moonstone was returned to the Daziarn. The Shianti then moved south to the Isle of Lorn. They encircled their new home with a web of enchantments, magical mists and mage winds to prevent man from ever finding their place of refuge in the Sea of Dreams. Knowledge of the Shianti faded with time, save in southern Magnamund where it became enshrined in legend, and the worship of them endured. Priests of the Shianti religion preserved their teachings and patiently awaited the day when the 'ancient ones' would return, bringing with them lasting peace and the blessing of a new golden age.

Two thousand years strode by and man advanced as Ishir had foretold. He built great cities and cultivated the land; his kingdoms rose and fell; he made war and loved and laughed and became master of his fate. But a new power was emerging in the province of Shadaki. There Shasarak the evil Wytch-king ruled. The black necromancer commanded an army of brutal soldiers and had a devoted following of men who upheld his religion of demonic worship and sacrificial rites. Devotees of the Shianti and other

11

religious cults were persecuted in a merciless purge. Ruthlessly, the Wytch-king destroyed all his opponents and began a terrible war with the peoples of the neighbouring provinces. From the ruins of war Shasarak shaped the Shadakine Empire, subjugating whole nations to his evil rule. And as the provinces fell to his might, the Shianti looked on helplessly, bound by their vow to the Goddess Ishir never to interfere in the affairs of man.

On the night of the crowning of Shasarak as Overlord of the Shadakine Empire, a great storm broke upon the Sea of Dreams, a storm that raged with unnatural intensity. Lashed by wind and rain, illuminated by wild lightning, the waters heaved and danced in fury to the thundering music of the storm, unchecked by even the enchantments of the Shianti. When finally the tempest died, the Shianti looked out in amazement on the shattered hull of a ship drifting towards their shore. Never before had this occurred, for the enchantments and mage winds had kept them secure from the curiosity of man by forcing him to sail close to his own land.

The Shianti went quickly to the ruined ship where they found only one survivor – a baby. They perceived the sudden arrival of this human child as a sign of great portent, and they conceived a plan by which they might lawfully aid mankind. They named the orphan child Grey Star, because a star is the symbol of hope in the Shianti faith, and because of the silver streak in the child's jet-black hair. In the shadow of the wrath of the Goddess Ishir, they raised the child as one of their own and taught him their secrets. Diligently they set about their instruction, for their aim was to provide a saviour for mankind. Armed with the might of Shianti wizardry and wisdom, their hope was to create an adversary equal in power to the evil Wytch-king of Shadaki, for they realized that only with the death of Shasarak would man once more be free to determine his destiny.

THE STORY SO FAR . . .

You are Grey Star, trained in the secret arts of a Shianti wizard. Sixteen years have passed since you arrived on the Isle of Lorn, the hidden realm of the Shianti race, when you are called to a meeting of your Shianti masters.

'Grey Star,' says Acarya, High Wizard of the Shianti, 'you have been summoned to this meeting so that we may lay before you a quest of great importance. Your people, the race of man, are slaves of an evil tyrant, Shasarak the Wytch-king of Shadaki. He has made pacts with demons and has captured the spirits of the dead who do his bidding as undead slaves. He has the power to control the minds of men; none can resist him and the land of your birth cries out in fear of the cruel hand that crushes its heart. No power remains intact to challenge the might of the Wytch-king. Our ancient vow to the Goddess Ishir forbids us from intervening in the fate of man, and the Moon-stone now lies hidden on another plane. We have taught you the ways of Shianti magic in the hope that one day you would take up this quest – to recover the Moonstone and use its power to destroy the Wytch-king. You are human. No vow prohibits you from leaving the Isle of Lorn, nor are you forbidden to aid mankind in any way you choose. No charge is laid upon you to accept the quest, yet if you refuse, your people will be doomed to a choice between slavery and destruction at the hands of the Wytch-king of Shadaki.'

Bravely and without hesitation, you give Acarya your decision, but your voice trembles as you speak: 'I accept the quest of the Moonstone. What must I do?'

There are sighs of relief all round. 'You have made us proud this day, son of man,' says Acarya, smiling. 'The Moonstone lies hidden in the Daziarn plane, which can only be entered by locating its portal. We know this can be found in the lands of men: it is called the "Shadow Gate". However, it rarely remains in any one location for more than a day and is invisible to human sight. For this reason you must seek out the Lost Tribe of Lara, a race of primitive but magical creatures we call the Kundi. They possess the gift of astral vision, which enables them to see the "Shadow Gate". Once, long ago, the Kundi inhabited the forests and mountains of Lara. Before the Shadakine army invaded the free provinces of the south, they passed through the mountains of Lara, using the Morn Pass. There the Shadakine army were frequently ambushed and delayed by the Kundi, who always disappeared into the safety of the forests before the Shadakine could retaliate. Finally, in desperation, the Wytch-king burnt the forests, and the Kundi were forced to flee. To this day no one is sure where the Kundi went, and consequently men refer to them as the Lost Tribe of Lara. Your first task is to find the lost tribe and persuade them to guide you to the Shadow Gate. Your training is incomplete but you must begin without delay. The Shadakine Empire now stretches to the very shores of the Sea of

15

Dreams, and the power of the Wytch-king grows with each passing day. Our presence is known to him and his attention is often turned towards us, probing our defences and testing the measure of our powers. He is hungry for new conquest, and though he fears us, the day is sure to come when he will cross the Sea of Dreams to challenge the Shianti.'

Acarya places his hands upon your shoulders and looks deeply into your eyes, 'The fate of humanity and of the Shianti depends on the success of your quest. Find the Moonstone, Grey Star . . . You are our only hope; if you fail then all is lost.'

THE GAME RULES

To keep a record of your adventure, use the *Action Chart* at the front of this book. If you run out of space, you can copy out the chart or have it photocopied.

Before you set off on your adventure, you must discover how well your Shianti masters have prepared you for your quest by determining your fighting prowess – COMBAT SKILL – your state of mind – WILLPOWER – and your physical stamina – ENDURANCE. To do this take a pencil and, with eyes closed, point with the blunt end of it on to the *Random Number Table* on the last page of this book. If you pick *0* it counts as zero.

The first number that you pick from the *Random Number Table* in this way represents your COMBAT SKILL. Add 10 to the number you picked and write the total in the COMBAT SKILL section of your *Action Chart*. (eg, if your pencil fell on the number 4 in the *Random Number Table* you would write in a COMBAT SKILL of 14.) When you fight, your COMBAT SKILL will be pitted against that of your enemy. A high score in this section is therefore very desirable.

The second number that you pick from the *Random Number Table* represents your WILLPOWER. Add 20 to this number and write the total in the WILLPOWER section of your *Action Chart* (eg, if your pencil fell on the number 6 in the *Random Number Table* you would have a WILLPOWER of 26). If you decide to use a spell or utilize the power of your Wizard's Staff, then you will lose WILLPOWER points. If at any time your WILLPOWER falls to zero, you may not use any of your spells or your Wizard's Staff. Lost WILLPOWER points can be regained during the course of the adventure and it is possible for your WILLPOWER points to rise above the total with which you start your adventure.

The third number that you pick from the *Random Number Table* represents your powers of ENDURANCE. Add 20 to this number and write the total in the ENDURANCE section of your *Action Chart* (eg, if your pencil fell on the number 6 on the *Random Number Table* you would have 26 ENDURANCE points). If you are wounded in combat, you will lose ENDURANCE points. If at any time your ENDURANCE points fall to zero, you are dead and the adventure is over. Lost ENDURANCE points can be regained during the course of the adventure but can never rise above the number with which you start your adventure.

MAGICAL POWERS

When you start your adventure, your education in the ways of wizardry is incomplete. You have mastered only *five* of the seven magical powers that the Shianti call the *lesser magicks*. The choice of which five powers these are, is up to you. All of the lesser magicks will be of use to you at some point on your quest, so choose them with care. Your survival may depend on the correct use of a magical power at the right time.

The seven magical powers available to you are listed below. When you have chosen your five powers, enter them in the Magical Powers section of your *Action Chart*.

This power allows a wizard to transform his thoughts or desires into magical energy. By concentration of the will it is possible to create magical shields of force to bar doors or move objects. Sorcery drains more WILLPOWER points than any other Magical Power, and is most effective when your WILLPOWER points are high.

If you choose this power, write 'Sorcery' on your *Action Chart*.

Enchantment.

The power of Enchantment enables a wizard to charm or beguile other creatures, and create illusions in the minds of others. He will be able to extract information from others, place thoughts and compulsions into another's mind or cause them to believe that imaginary events are actually taking place. Some magical or highly intelligent beings may be immune to the powers of Enchantment.

If you choose this power, write 'Enchantment' on your *Action Chart*.

Elementalism

The Power of elemental magic allows a wizard some control over the natural elements of Air, Fire, Earth and Water. By entering a trance and chanting incantations, you may summon aid from the spirits of the Elemental Plane. Elementals have very little understanding of man, and for this reason a wizard can never be sure of the nature of the aid the Elementals may send.

If you choose this power, write 'Elementalism' on your *Action Chart*.

A wizard who possesses the power of Alchemy is able, through the mixing of various substances, to create magical potions. Given the correct ingredients, a potion may restore lost energy (ie, ENDURANCE points, WILLPOWER), or temporarily improve various abilities (eg, COMBAT SKILL). The use of alchemy may also allow a wizard to alter the nature of substances (eg, change lead into gold), but the necessary ingredients and the correct equipment (eg, a pestle and mortar) must be at hand. The use of the power of Alchemy drains no WILLPOWER.

If you choose this power write 'Alchemy' on your *Action Chart*.

The power of prophecy allows a wizard to fortell the future through meditation. A meditative state will allow a wizard to make the correct decision when facing conflicting choices or difficult actions; to discover the whereabouts of a person he has once met, or an object he has once seen. It may also allow him to determine the true nature of a stranger or a strange object. Magical beings or objects are sometimes hidden from the power of prophecy.

If you choose this power, write 'Prophecy' on your *Action Chart*.

This power bestows upon a wizard the ability to deduce facts about events by touching objects connected to them. Through deep concentration, a wizard may lay his hands upon any inanimate object

22

and visualize scenes that have affected it. Visions brought about through the use of Psychomancy are often cryptic, taking the form of a riddle or puzzle. Some magic items are resistant to the use of Psychomancy and may, sometimes, impart misleading information.

If you choose this power, write 'Psychomancy' on your *Action Chart*.

Mastery of this power permits contact with the spirit realm. A wizard wishing to speak with the dead, or to call up a form from the spirit world, must draw a magic pentacle and enter a trance, when the use of the correct spell-chant will reach out to the Spiritual Plane. Standing within the protection of a magic pentacle, a wizard may consider himself to be relatively safe from harm. If he wishes to speak with a corpse, especially one whose former life was good and righteous, then a wizard can expect help and advice. However, contact with those whose former lives were evil or selfish can be a perilous, and often fatal, experience. Evil spirits are reluctant to return to the realm of the dead and may try to trick a wizard into freeing them into the world of the living. All spirits, good and evil, will require some service of the wizard in return for their aid. Any failure to perform this task, however difficult, may result in the wizard losing his life.

If you choose this power, write 'Evocation' on your *Action Chart*.

Your Staff is your most valuable possession. It looks and feels like an ordinary quarterstaff yet it is stronger than any known metal. This is your main combat weapon, for you are untrained in the use of any other form of armed combat. It contains a potent force that is unleashed at will by the power of your mind, and causes a beam of destructive power to hurtle from its tip. Every time you unleash this power you must deduct 1 WILLPOWER point.

In the event that your enemy survives such an attack or should you fall victim to a surprise attack, you will be forced to engage in close combat and must attempt to strike your enemy with the Staff. If your attack is successful, a bolt of energy will be released from the Staff that is capable of inflicting great physical harm. If you wish to increase the amount of damage that you inflict in this way, you must use more WILLPOWER points and multiply the number of

ENDURANCE points lost by the enemy, accordingly. For example, if you chose to expend 3 WILLPOWER points on your attack, all enemy ENDURANCE point losses would be multiplied by three.

If you enter combat without your Staff, deduct 6 points from your COMBAT SKILL. If you have no weapon at all, you must deduct 8 points from your COMBAT SKILL.

EQUIPMENT

You wear the grey robe and hooded cloak of a Shianti Wizard. Your only weapon is your Wizard's Staff (note this on your *Action Chart* under Weapons). You wear a Backpack containing 4 Meals (note under Meals on your *Action Chart*), and you have been given a map of the Shadakine Empire (note under Special Items on your *Action Chart*) which you place inside your robe.

If you have chosen Alchemy as one of your Magical Powers, then you will have a leather pouch for herbs and potions hanging from your belt. The Herb Pouch contains the following:

2 empty vials for carrying potions
1 vial containing saltpetre
1 vial containing sulphur
Mark these 4 items in your *Action Chart*.
Your Herb Pouch will carry a maximum of six items.

On your last day on the Isle of Lorn, your Shianti Masters offer you the following gifts to aid you in your quest. According to Shianti custom, you may choose one of them. They are:

JEWELLED DAGGER (Special Item). This adds 1 point to your COMBAT SKILL when used in combat.

MAGIC TALISMAN (Special Item). This adds 2 points to your WILLPOWER total.

VIAL OF LAUMSPUR (Backpack Item). This restores 4 ENDURANCE points to your total when swallowed after combat. There is enough for one dose.

When you have made your choice, mark the item on your *Action Chart* under the headings given in brackets, and make a note of any effect it may have on your ENDURANCE, WILLPOWER or COMBAT SKILL totals.

How to carry equipment

Now that you have your equipment, the following list shows you how it is carried. You do not need to make notes but you can refer back to this list in the course of your adventure.

WIZARD'S STAFF – carried in the hand.
BACKPACK – slung over the shoulder.
MEALS – carried in the Backpack.
JEWELLED DAGGER – tucked into your belt.
MAGIC TALISMAN – worn on a chain around your neck.
VIAL OF LAUMSPUR – carried in the Backpack.

How much can you carry?

Weapons

The maximum number of weapons that you may carry is *two*. Your Wizard's Staff counts as one weapon.

Backpack Items

These must be stored in your Backpack. Because space is limited, you may only keep a maximum of eight articles, including Meals, in your Backpack at any one time.

Special Items

Special Items are not carried in the Backpack. When you discover a Special Item, you will be told how to carry it.

Nobles (Shadakine currency)

These are carried in your Belt Pouch.

Food

Food is carried in your Backpack. Each Meal counts as one item.

Any item that may be of use and can be picked up on your adventure and entered on your *Action Chart* is given capital letters in the text. Unless you are told it is a Special Item, carry it in your Backpack.

How to use your equipment

Weapons

Your COMBAT SKILL depends on your Wizard's Staff. If you do not possess your Staff when you enter combat you must deduct 6 points from your COMBAT SKILL. If you enter a combat without a weapon, deduct 8 points from your COMBAT SKILL and fight with your bare hands. If you find a weapon during the adventure, you may pick it up and use it. (Remember that you can only carry *two* weapons at once.)

Backpack Items

During your travels you will discover various useful items which you may wish to keep. (Remember that you can only carry a maximum of eight items in your Backpack at any one time.) You may exchange or discard them at any point when you are not involved in combat.

Special Items

Each Special Item has a particular purpose or effect. You may be told this when the item is discovered, or it may be revealed to you as the adventure progresses.

Currency

The currency of the Shadakine Empire is the Noble, which is a small jade stone. The system of money is alien to the Shianti and for this reason you begin your adventure with no money. Whenever you kill an enemy, you may take any Nobles belonging to him and keep them in your Belt Pouch.

Food

You will need to eat regularly during your adventure. If you do not have any food when you are instructed to eat a Meal, you will lose 3 ENDURANCE points.

RULES FOR COMBAT

There will be occasions during your adventure when you have to fight an enemy. The enemy's COMBAT SKILL and ENDURANCE points are given in the text. Grey Star's aim during the combat is to kill the enemy by reducing his ENDURANCE points to zero while at the same time losing as few ENDURANCE points as possible himself.

At the start of a combat, enter Grey Star's ENDURANCE and WILLPOWER points and the enemy's ENDURANCE points in the appropriate boxes on the Combat Record section of your *Action Chart*.

The sequence for combat is as follows:

1. Calculate your current COMBAT SKILL total, based on the weapon you are using. (Remember, if you enter combat without your Staff, you must deduct 6 points from your COMBAT SKILL. If you have no weapon at all, you must deduct 8 points.)

2. Subtract the COMBAT SKILL of your enemy from this total. The result is your *Combat Ratio*. Enter it on the *Action Chart*.

3. If you are using your Wizard's Staff, decide how many WILLPOWER points you wish to use. (Remember, you must expend at least 1 point.) Enter this number on your Combat Record in the box marked WILLPOWER.

Example

Grey Star (COMBAT SKILL 15, WILLPOWER 23) is ambushed by a Deathgaunt (COMBAT SKILL 20). He is not given the opportunity to evade combat, but he can use his Wizard's Staff against the creature as it swoops down on him. He subtracts the Deathgaunt's COMBAT SKILL from his own, giving a *Combat Ratio* of −5. (15 − 20 = −5).

−5 is noted on the *Action Chart* as the *Combat Ratio*. Grey Star decides to use 2 WILLPOWER points, which is noted on the WILLPOWER box of the Combat Record.

4. When you have decided upon the number of WILLPOWER points you wish to use, and have determined your *Combat Ratio,* pick a number from the *Random Number Table.*

5. Turn to the *Combat Results Table* on the inside back cover of the book. Along the top of the chart are shown the *Combat Ratio* numbers. Find the number that is the same as your *Combat Ratio* and cross-reference it with the random number that you have picked. (The random numbers appear on the side of the chart.) You now have the number of ENDURANCE points lost by Grey Star. To calculate the number lost by the enemy, multiply this by the number of WILLPOWER points that Grey Star elected to use. Now you have the final number of ENDURANCE points lost by both Grey Star and his enemy in this round of combat. (*E* represents points lost by the enemy; *GS* represents points lost by Grey Star.)

Example
The *Combat Ratio* between Grey Star and the Deathgaunt has been established as −5, and Grey Star's WILLPOWER points used as 2. If the number taken from the *Random Number Table* is a 6, then the result of the first round of combat is:

Grey Star loses 4 ENDURANCE points.
Deathgaunt loses 5 ENDURANCE points, multiplied by 2 WILLPOWER points, giving a total of 10 ENDURANCE points lost in all.

6. On the *Action Chart*, mark the changes in ENDURANCE points to the participants in the combat, and Grey Star's amended WILLPOWER points total.

7. Unless otherwise instructed, or unless you have an option to evade, the next round of combat now starts.

8. Repeat the sequence from Stage 3.

This process of combat continues until the ENDURANCE points of either the enemy or Grey Star are reduced to zero, at which point the one with the zero score is declared dead. If Grey Star is dead, the adventure is over. If the enemy is dead, Grey Star proceeds but with his ENDURANCE and WILLPOWER points reduced.

A summary of Combat Rules appears on the page after the *Random Number Table*.

Evasion of combat
During your adventure you may be given the chance to evade combat. If you have already engaged in a round of combat and decide to evade, calculate the combat for that round in the usual manner. All points lost by the enemy as a result of that round are

31

ignored, and you make your escape. Only Grey Star may lose ENDURANCE points during that round, but then that is the risk of running away! You may only evade if the text of the particular section allows you to do so.

SAGE ADVICE

You are about to embark on a quest of great peril, for your journey will take you to an unknown land that is dominated by evil. Refer to the map at the front of this book and make notes as you progress through the story: they are sure to be of great help to you in future adventures.

You will discover items that could be of help to you on your quest. Some Special Items may aid you in future Grey Star adventures, others may be red herrings of no real use at all, so be selective in what you decide to keep.

Be cautious in your use of WILLPOWER points, as your WILLPOWER is the energy source for your Magical Powers and your Wizard's Staff. A score of zero WILLPOWER points will leave you weak and vulnerable to attack, unable to offer effective resistance.

Follow the path of wisdom, Wizard Grey Star. The way of fools is the road to destruction.

Good luck!

Grey Star the Wizard

It is a grim, chill morning, your last on the Isle of Lorn. With quaking heart, you enter the sacred temple of Amida to receive the silent blessing of your Shianti masters. They stand around you, heads bowed in meditation. At length, the ceremony ends and Maiteya, your old friend and teacher, steps forward, and grasps you firmly by the shoulders. You look into his glittering eyes and see yourself reflected there, for the eyes of the Shianti race are not coloured like man's but have pupils that cast reflections like mirrored glass.

'Grey Star,' he says, a warm smile lighting his serene face, 'the time has come for you to leave. Far will you travel and perilous is your course. Be not afraid, yet do not fear caution. Though you go with the teaching and blessing of the Shianti and carry the might of the Wizard's Staff, stealth and secrecy will be your allies. Let not courage defeat wisdom. Go now and seek the Kundi race that are called the Lost Tribe of Lara. You are the instrument of our will, bearer of our hope. Ever will your quest be in our minds and hearts.'

Without a word, you turn and leave the temple, not looking back until you reach the shore, where a sail boat awaits you. With a gentle sigh, you bid farewell to the island of your youth and push the little craft into the cold waters of the Sea of Dreams. You jump into the boat and set sail, making a westward course for the distant mainland of the Shadakine Empire.

I. With quaking heart you enter the sacred temple of
Amida

If you have the Magical Power of Elementalism and wish to use it to aid your voyage, turn to **202**.

If you do not possess this power, or do not wish to use it, turn to **168**.

2

The way leads south through the farms and paddy fields of the region. The path keeps firmly to the line of the Azan River as it curves towards the great Azagad Gorge, a great pitted canyon of weathered limestone columns. In order to maintain the secrecy of your presence, you avoid the homesteads that nestle by the river.

You walk for two long days and must consume 2 Meals or lose 6 ENDURANCE points. The regulated squares of the rice fields become fewer and fewer, and finally give way to a flat expanse of unyielding plains called the Wilderwastes, which are devoid of human habitation. That night, you make camp on the leeward side of a small outcrop of hills.

Turn to **24**.

3

You leave the road and, after travelling a short way through the thickening trees, you discover a small clearing, sheltered by a large, overhanging Acacia tree.

You decide to rest here. You are hungry and must eat 1 Meal or lose 3 ENDURANCE points. Your remaining 2 Meals must be given to Tanith and Shan. (Remember to cross all these from your *Action Chart*.)

You have no blankets and dare not start a fire for fear

of revealing your hiding place but fortunately it is a warm night. Shan and Tanith insist that you sleep while they take it in turns to keep watch. Wryly, you point out that it is the first time that they have agreed about anything.

If you decide to take up their offer, turn to **85**.
If you would prefer to take the first watch, turn to **275**.

4

You vault on to the dead tree, using your Staff for support. Hauling yourself to the top, you reach out and grab the thick branch of a Giant Azawood. Your chest contracts with pain every time you draw breath and the humid, fetid air clings to the sides of your throat. Slowly and painfully, you climb the tall tree while the columns of insects march relentlessly towards you, their pincers gnashing and clacking in crazed fury.

Grimly you ignore the savage pain of your wounded leg. Looking up you gasp with dismay, for a line of Cave Mantiz has somehow gained the branch above your head. Those behind are nearly upon you, and in desperation you clamber along the nearest branch. The further you crawl along the narrowing tree limb, the greater the swaying of the branch as it bends under your weight.

You turn to see a line of insects scurrying along the branch towards you: there is no escape. With one last effort of will you use all your remaining WILLPOWER points in an attempt to clear the branch of the Cave Mantiz.

Turn to **350**.

5

You hurl a bolt from your Staff at the plant that threatens Shan. It is quickly destroyed by the searing blue flame, but the effort has cost you 2 WILLPOWER points.

Suddenly, you are aware that creepers are clutching at your legs. As you crash to the ground, a tendril coils around your throat and pulls you towards the poison barbs of another Yaku plant. You are being slowly strangled to death and must lose 3 ENDURANCE points.

Turn to **42**.

6

You push onwards into the heart of the 'Dragon's Teeth'. The sun beats savagely on your heads. You lose 4 ENDURANCE points due to heat exhaustion before you reach the far side of the gorge and sight the Great Wall of Azakawa.

7

In the evening light you regard with awe the towering cliff face, stretching like a vast curtain of rock from east to west as far as the eye can see.

You press on, anxious to reach the Azanam by nightfall.

Turn to **325**.

7

You learn that the girl's name is Tanith. She is a novice in the ways of witchcraft and is in the service of Mother Magri, her protector and guardian. She is very beautiful and has long, dark, unkempt hair and wild green eyes. 'They say that you are a wizard and that you challenged the truthsay of the Kazim Stone,' she says, curiously.

'Of course,' you reply, a little boastfully, wishing to impress this ragged but winsome creature.

'That is very bad,' she says, shaking her head. 'Mother Magri will have you tortured. The ways of the Shadaki are very cruel. Tonight, you will be taken to the Darkling Room and you will experience great pain and terror.'

'Then I must escape this place,' you say, fearfully. 'Can you help me?'

Tanith gazes at you, a frightened expression on her face. 'No . . . No . . . The danger . . . I cannot . . . I dare not!' She takes a dried flower from the pocket of her dress, and sprinkles its powdered petals into your food. 'This will help fortify you before your ordeal,' she explains, her voice trembling. 'I can do no more.'

She jumps to her feet. 'I'm sorry . . .' She falters, a longing note in her voice, and then she disappears.

Turn to **270**.

8

You crawl into the shelter of the tiny cave, scarcely large enough to contain you, and immediately notice a small tunnel leading upwards. The ghostly mist of Lake Shenwu lingers on the cave floor, dimly lighting the rough hewn ceiling and walls.

You are tired and need to sleep.

If you wish to sleep here, turn to **14**.
If you would rather enter the tunnel, turn to **19**.

9

Bravely you fight off the soldier Mantiz, but soon the whole nest is upon you and, in a matter of minutes, they have stripped your flesh to the bone.

Your life and your quest end tragically, here.

10

You get up and walk over to Tanith, who looks up with a startled expression.

'Grey Star,' she gasps, 'I . . . I could not resist. I am sorry . . .'

If you have the Kazim Stone of Mother Magri, turn to **51**.
If you do not, turn to **102**.

11

Before the Shadakine come any nearer, you loose a bolt of force from your Staff, killing one of them outright. The attack has cost you 1 WILLPOWER point. The remaining warrior hangs back. At first you think that he has simply lost his nerve, but then notice with sinking heart that more Shadakine are approaching from behind. They are armed with crossbows, which are aimed directly at you.

'Surrender or die,' shouts one of the Shadakine.

> If you wish to surrender, turn to **300**.
> If you decide to attack, turn to **66**.
> If you wish to turn and make a run for it, turn to **20**.

12

At the expense of 3 WILLPOWER points you are able to cut a path through the smoking remains of the Yaku. Soon you are completely free of them, and in the fading light you come within sight of the Great Wall of Azakawa.

Turn to **325**.

13

The forest is very near and it is a dark night. Fortunately, you have not been seen. Diving into the undergrowth at the forest's edge you lie as still as possible as the Shadakine chariot rattles past at breakneck speed. The vicious blades on the wheel hubs flash as the chariot passes dangerously close to your hiding place.

You wait with baited breath for several minutes after it has passed but the chariot does not return.

Turn to **75**.

14

It is a sleep from which you will not awaken. The poisonous mist overwhelms you as you slumber. The cave has become your tomb and your body will never be found.

You have failed in your quest.

15

You leave the Chansi Hills far behind and cross the Suhni River once more, following its winding course through the dense forest. Tanith continues to summon small game, a sight which you still find disturbing. Shan leads you through the forest, but this time you encounter no Shadakine patrols.

You are not required to exert any Magical Power and may restore ENDURANCE and WILLPOWER points to the value of one half your current totals. (Remember that unlike your WILLPOWER total, your ENDURANCE points total may never exceed the number with which you started your adventure.)

Turn to **218**.

16

When you agree to the paltry price of 20 Nobles, the old man brightens visibly. He hands you the 20 jade stones and you place them in your Belt Pouch. Mark these on your *Action Chart*.

You try to coax some information from him and ask about the legend of the Lost Tribe of Lara. However, he is reluctant to talk, looking away from you and shifting uneasily from one foot to the other, seemingly anxious to be gone.

'Try the Inn of the Laughing Moon at the end of yonder street,' he mutters finally. 'You'll find plenty of traveller's talk there.'

Following the direction of his finger, you see a dark, narrow street leading from the harbour area. When you turn back to face him, you find that you are alone. The old man has disappeared into the night.

If you want to enter the narrow street, turn to **200**.
If you would rather explore the harbour front, turn to **100**.

17

You step into the thick, muddy water and immediately scream in pain. Your flesh feels as if it is on fire. You fall head first into the poisonous waters of Lake Shenwu and in a matter of minutes you have drowned.

Lake Shenwu has claimed another victim and you have failed in your quest.

18 – *Illustration II (overleaf)*

It appears your new companions put great faith in your leadership; a faith that is only slightly shaken when you admit that you have very little idea of where to go. You explain that your quest is to find the Lost Tribe of Lara (though you do not tell them its origin or true purpose), and suggest that Shan guides you. 'There is no obligation upon you to remain with me, though,' you tell Tanith and Shan. 'You are free to do as you please.'

'I for one have no other place to go,' says Tanith. 'Mother Magri was a cruel mistress and I would gladly aid any opponent of the rule of the Wytch-king and his servants.'

'And I too,' says Shan. 'But which way shall we go? We must keep moving for it is certain that the Shadakine are searching for us.'

There is a pause while you all consider the problem. Finally you ask if they have any suggestions. Shan's advice is to journey south to the Azanam, which he believes to be the most likely haunt of the lost tribe, and he offers to guide you there.

'But if you are wrong,' says Tanith, 'We will have journeyed far and into great danger unnecessarily. We need guidance. Three days' travel to the north of here lives Jnana the Wise, a hermit sage, "He Who Serves No Master". I can take you to him.'

II.   There is a pause while you all consider the problem

If you have the Medallion of the 'Redeemer', turn to **264**.

If you decide to take Shan's advice, turn to **190**.

If you wish to seek the counsel of Jnana the Wise, turn to **134**.

19

The tunnel is very narrow and you have to crawl on your hands and knees. It slopes gently upwards, and as you continue your body is squeezed tighter and tighter between the smooth stone walls. You feel that you must soon suffocate in the claustrophobic darkness. Then finally and with great relief, you reach the end of the tunnel and pull yourself through, panting and sweating.

It is still pitch dark, but you are able to stand, and you sense that you are in some kind of cavern.

If you have a Torch and Tinderbox and wish to light the Torch in order to take a look around, turn to **35**.

If you would rather exert 1 WILLPOWER point to create a small glow from your Wizard's Staff, turn to **46**.

If you do not have either of these Items, or do not wish to use them, turn to **59**.

20

You are left with only seconds in which to regret your foolish decision. The Shadakine warriors do not feel the least compunction about shooting a man in the back and your body is soon fatally punctured by a crossbow bolt.

Your life and your quest end here.

21

You journey along the road and, to Shan's surprise, discover that it is deserted. 'I can't understand it,' he says, puzzled. 'This road is usually teeming with traders.'

You have been walking for three hours when you sight a wagon parked by the roadside. A group of men are sitting around a camp fire near a small grove of trees. 'Wait here,' says Shan. 'I'll see if I can get some information out of these merchants about the road that lies ahead.'

He returns shortly, carrying a shortsword. He smiles broadly. 'A bargain,' he says. 'Only 5 Nobles. It must be worth at least 20. Always ready to strike a bargain with a fool,' he beams.

'What about the road?' asks Tanith, impatiently. 'Why is it empty?'

'The Shadakine are searching for us,' he replies. 'The roads and bridges have been closed until they discover us. These merchants were stranded and have made camp.'

'We'll have to keep to the cover of the forest from now on,' you say, worried. You enter the forest and continue your journey cautiously.

Turn to **39**.

22

You run up the curving tunnel but are forced to stop after a little way. The low-ceilinged passage is now in total darkness and you cannot even see your hand stretched out before your face.

If you have a Torch and Tinderbox, you may light the Torch to help you to see your way. If you do not have a Torch, or would prefer not to use it, you may expend 1 WILLPOWER point creating a light from the tip of your Wizard's Staff. This light will last until you extinguish it and you will not have to use any more WILLPOWER points to keep it alight.

If you choose to continue in darkness, turn to **122**.
If you choose to light your way, turn to **334**.

23

Stepping as lightly as you can, you turn right, with Shan following close behind. At the end of the corridor are two stairways both leading upwards.

If you have the power of Prophecy and wish to use it, turn to **92**. (Note this section number first as you will need to return to it later.)
If you wish to take the left stairway, turn to **137**.
If you wish to take the right stairway, turn to **321**.

24

You fall into an uneasy sleep in which you are troubled by strange dreams. You wake with a start in the middle of the night to see Tanith crouched over the dying embers of the camp-fire, which glows with a dull, yellow light.

If you wish to investigate, turn to **10**.
If you wish to pretend that you are sleeping, turn to **33**.

25

You recognize the small ante-chamber. It was here that Mother Magri subjected you to the test of truth, using the Kazim Stone. The terrible glowing sphere stands in the centre of the empty room on a small table; it is giving off a faint light.

If you wish to take the Kazim Stone, turn to **77**.
If you wish to leave the ante-chamber immediately, turn to **129**.

26

Glancing behind, you notice a small, weasel-faced man ducking in and out of the shadows cast by the flickering torchlight. You are being followed.

If you wish to act as if nothing has happened, turn to **97**.
If you wish to confront the weasel-faced man, turn to **166**.
If you would prefer to leave the market square and make a run for it, turn to **241**.

27

With your Staff still crackling with wild energy, illuminating the alley-way, you turn around and run towards the narrow street for all you are worth.

Turn to **195**.

28

In one swift, fluid movement, you rise to stand upon the shoulders of those who bear you. The mob lets out a rousing cheer that peters into silence as you dive into the mass of people packed tightly behind you. Your fall is cushioned by their bodies and unharmed you quickly scramble to your feet.

You hear the unmistakable sound of people crying out in pain as two Shadakine warriors beat a bloody path through the human wall that separates them from you.

If you wish to aid the people you have just deserted, turn to **308**.

If you would rather escape under the cover of the ensuing chaos, turn to **336**.

29 – *Illustration III (overleaf)*

As the river begins to narrow, the once clear waters of the Azan River become a murky brown. Close to the banks, there are many shallow inlets where stagnant pools and swamps are overgrown with clumps of rope-like tendrils. These tendrils form the branches of a large plant called the Yaku. The tendrils are sensitized vines that snake across the ground towards a pool or into the main river, for the rest of the limestone canyon is arid. At the heart of the Yaku plant is

III. Stagnant pools and swamps are overgrown with clumps of rope-like tendrils

a cluster of sharp points, and Shan warns you to keep well clear of these poisoned barbs.

It becomes increasingly hard to remain close to the river's edge without clusters of Yaku tendrils blocking your path.

> If you wish to move further away from the Azan River and the difficult ground that borders it, turn to **54**.
>
> If you would prefer to keep to the river, thus following a direct path to the Wall of Azakawa and the cloud forests of the Azanam that lie beyond, turn to **104**.

30

It is impossible to see which Yaku stem the tendrils are attached to, so you attack the wriggling cluster with a wide, sweeping stroke of your Staff across them all; you exert 2 WILLPOWER points.

You have made the right decision; you have severed all the tendrils that threatened you. You are safe . . . for the moment.

Turn to **128**.

31

You are very tired. Wearily, you close your eyes and call on the Elementals for their aid. Your chant ends and at first it seems that you have failed. Then you hear the sound of rushing water: a gigantic wave rises up further along the river. The foaming white crest of the wave towers above the bridge in the shape of an outstretched hand. The watery fingers clench to form an immense fist that smashes on to the bridge, crushing it as though it were made of matchsticks, and drenching the three of you, as it washes the bridge downstream.

'Such power!' Tanith exclaims, her eyes shining with childish delight and admiration.

The spell has cost you 1 WILLPOWER point.

Turn to **75**.

32

Skilfully you wield your Staff, shielding yourself from the creature's deadly touch as it passes overhead. You watch as the Quoku climbs in the sky, flying in a wide circle to position itself for its next attack.

Suddenly, the Quoku dives towards Shan.

If you wish to attempt a long range attack on the Quoku, turn to **107**.

If you wish to try to defend Shan from the attack, turn to **57**.

33

Tanith is talking quietly, addressing her words to the fire. 'No Mother, I will not . . . I cannot . . .' A diminutive figure shivering by the dwindling fire, she is obviously greatly distressed. Perhaps her conscience troubles her?

If you have the Kazim Stone, turn to **51**.

If you wish to investigate, turn to **10**.

If you wish to leave Tanith to the privacy of her own thoughts, turn to **69**.

34

The alley is deserted. Peering into the dark shadows you step cautiously into the darkness. Suddenly you are grabbed from behind and a knife is held at your throat.

'Turn around,' a voice whispers, menacingly, 'Slowly, or I'll cut your throat. Then hand over your money.'

Slowly you turn to face the shabby thief.

> If you do not have any money, or have money but do not wish to hand it over, turn to **76**.
> If you prefer to hand over your money, turn to **133**.

35

In the flaring light you see a narrow chamber with smooth walls. It looks like neither a natural cavern, nor like anything a man might carve. The floor is strewn with dead leaves, twigs, a few scattered bones and ancient dust. Leading from the cavern is another tunnel, slightly wider than the one you have just come through. A cool breeze is coming from it, and freshens the musty air.

You are falling asleep on your feet, and throwing caution to the wind you decide that you will rest here, for the cavern looks as if it has been deserted for a very long time. You extinguish your light and lie down to sleep.

Turn to **59**.

'My name is Tanith,' the girl announces. 'What's yours?' You tell her your name, still stunned at her apparent coldness.

'I am learning the ways of witchcraft in the service of Mother Magri,' she continues. 'She says you're a wizard; is that true?'

'Of course,' you reply, a little boastfully. For some reason, you wish to impress this beautiful young girl with wild, unkempt hair, all ragged and black, and penetrating, green eyes.

'That is very bad. Mother Magri will have you tortured as an enemy of the Wytch-king. She will take you to the Darkling Room.'

'Then I must escape,' you blurt out. 'Can you help me?'

'I've often dreamed of leaving here,' she says wistfully. 'Perhaps you could take me with you?'

'Yes . . . yes,' you say, willing her to aid you. She pauses, a blank expression on her face. 'But it would take more than a boy and a fat man to do that,' she snaps angrily, suddenly breaking into peals of girlish laughter. And she flounces away wearing a smug expression, and leaving you with your hopes shattered.

'She must have come to taunt us,' says Shan. 'Such spiteful people these Shadakine!' You finish your food and try to conceive a plan that will gain your freedom.

If you wish to try to sleep in order to build up your strength, turn to **201**.

If you do not wish to sleep, turn to **144**.

37

A quick search of the body reveals the jailer's Keys (a Special Item which you carry in your hand) and 3 Nobles. You may keep these Items and also his Dagger if you wish. Remember to mark them on your *Action Chart*.

There is no other exit from this room and you head back towards the other stairway.

Turn to **137**.

38

For three days you trace a path along the Suhni River as it winds through the heart of the forest. You carry no provisions, but Tanith is able to provide food for you all. She displays an uncanny control over animals, calling to the mesmerized creatures in a strange language and then coolly wringing their necks.

On your journey you manage to avoid the frequent Shadakine patrols that dog your path, and as you are not required to use any magic you may restore 2 WILLPOWER and 4 ENDURANCE points to your current totals.

You discover clumps of the Laumspur herb growing along the river and decide to pick some of it. If you have the Magical Power of Alchemy you may store it in your Herb Pouch. Remember to mark the Laumspur on your *Action Chart*. Swallowing it will regain 4 ENDURANCE points. If you do not have the power of Alchemy you must swallow the Laumspur while it is fresh to regain 4 ENDURANCE points and may not store it.

As you are picking the Laumspur, three Shadakine warriors burst out of the forest. You have been ambushed.

Turn to **117**.

39 – *Illustration IV*

Moving under cover of the forest's edge, Shan leads the way along a worn path. Unexpectedly, he stops, head tilted to one side, listening intently. 'What is it?' you whisper.

'I heard a shout, ahead of us. Listen!' In the distance you can hear angry voices and the ring of steel against steel. Cautiously, you creep forward and peer through the dense undergrowth.

Six armoured knights, clad in blue and red robes are battling with twenty Shadakine warriors. The knights are defending a heavily laden wagon that stands in the middle of a wide stone bridge. Perched on the wagon sits an unarmed man, richly clothed, looking fearfully upon the battle. He and his knights are outnumbered. Though skilled swordsmen, as the many Shadakine dead attest, they are hard-pressed, and have little chance of holding the bridge.

'They don't stand a chance,' you murmur.

'But these are no ordinary soldiers,' replies Shan. 'Look at the design on their shields – a mountain crowned with two stars. They bear the Royal Arms of Durenor. These are Knights of the White Mountain,

IV.   The knights are defending a heavily laden wagon

warrior lords of Durenor, a free kingdom in the far north.'

If you are to continue your journey south along the Azan River, you will have to somehow pass this battle without the Shadakine seeing you.

If you wish to go to the aid of the Knights of the White Mountain, turn to **55**.

If you wish to try to skirt around the battle and cross the road, turn to **208**.

40

You dash away from the harbour and along the narrow street, darting like a hunted beast among the doorways and shadows. Tall warehouse buildings rise up on either side of the street and the only sound you can hear is that of your own footsteps.

You have run only a short way when you reach a crossroads. The right and left turnings lead into alleyways, while the narrow street continues ahead.

If you have the Magical Power of Prophecy and wish to use it, turn to **64**.

If you wish to turn into the left alley-way, turn to **223**.

If you wish to turn into the right alley-way, turn to **76**.

If you would rather continue along the narrow street, turn to **195**.

41

You are running down a long winding passage. There are many doors leading from the corridor but you have no way of knowing which to open. You look ahead and a chill runs down your spine. At the far end of the passage you see someone approaching, wielding a tall staff.

Turn to **349**.

42

You are now held by an ever-increasing number of creepers that curl around your body. With cries of frustration, Shan slices away the creeper that is wound round your neck and arms. But he fears he is fighting a futile battle, for the poison barbs of the Yaku plant wave inches from your face. You are both enmeshed in a web of tightening vines. To your dismay, you lose hold of your Wizard's Staff, and watch helplessly as it rolls out of reach. You must make a life or death decision and only seconds remain.

If you possess the Jewelled Dagger of your Shianti Masters, and wish to strike at the Yaku plant before it impales you upon its poison barbs, turn to **216**.

If you possess any other Weapon (other than your Staff) and wish to attack the crimson heart of the Yaku, turn to **262**.

If you wish to tell Shan to plunge his sword into the Yaku plant, turn to **119**.

43

The lake is very wide. The roar from the Shenwu Falls is deafening. The waters fall hundreds of feet before cascading into the swirling currents below. Beyond the area of the waterfall the lake is strangely still. A writhing mist hangs suspended in the air. The mist is strangely luminous and allows you to see the foul yellow water beneath. Around the edge of the lake, the ground is completely bare; you cannot see a single living thing. You empty Shan's Backpack and discover the following items:

Enough food for 3 Meals
1 small vial of Laumspur (restores 2 ENDURANCE points)
2 Torches
1 Coil of Rope
A Tinderbox

If you wish to keep any of these Items, mark them on your *Action Chart*.

The mist gives off an acrid, choking vapour that racks your lungs. Coughing, you survey the sheer cliffs, towering ramparts of stone that stretch to the east and west in a vast semi-circle. Directly above these cliffs is the Azanam, your final goal.

If you have the power of Prophecy and wish to use it, turn to **143**.

If you wish to explore the basin and the area around Lake Shenwu, turn to **68**.

If you wish to try to find a way of scaling the cliffs, turn to **118**.

44

With an almighty blow, you cleave the skull of the Quoku in two. It emits a chilling shriek and falls back, writhing and twitching for a few seconds before finally expiring. But it is a hollow victory, for the lifeless body falls on to Shan's prone form.

If you wish to move the corpse of the Quoku, turn to **317**.

If you would rather continue your journey, skirting around the perilous ravine, turn to **335**.

45

You climb a short flight of stairs. At the top of the stairs is a closed wooden door. You can hear muffled conversation and sporadic laughter coming from behind the door.

If you wish to open the door, turn to **312**.

If you wish to head back and take the other stairway, turn to **80**.

46

Expending 1 WILLPOWER point, you cause the tip of your Wizard's Staff to glow; its eerie light sends shadows dancing across the walls and ceiling of the cavern. You see that the cavern is empty.

Turn to **35**.

47

Looking up, you see that the tunnel leads to an almost vertical shaft; the glare of sunlight blinds your eyes. Cursing breathlessly, you jump up and catch hold of a thick plant root protruding from the earth wall of the shaft and begin to climb. The narrow shaft is barely wide enough to let you pass and the climb is difficult and slow. Half-way up the shaft you cry out: you are stuck in a bottle-neck and can no longer move.

The first of the enraged soldier Mantiz enters the

shaft, and reaching out with its extended forelegs, it makes a grab for your flailing legs. A slash of burning pain ravages your right leg as a spurt of acid strips your calf to the bone. You lose 8 ENDURANCE points.

With a desperate cry you squeeze yourself through the gap and pull yourself free. Your leg is numb and hinders your climb, but with a superhuman effort you reach the top of the shaft. You have reached the surface at last and find yourself in a large clearing, surrounded by towering trees and dense, green foliage.

Turn to **146**.

48

The bridge covers a large area and the magic shield that you place over it costs you 3 WILLPOWER points. The extreme mental exertion has cost you dear. Your legs buckle under and you fall to the ground, barely conscious. Tanith and Shan pull you to your feet and half carry you into the shelter of the forest.

Turn to **75**.

49

You take a few deep breaths and then run towards the ravine. You hurl yourself off the edge, high into space, and sail over the yawning chasm. With limbs flailing and hands reaching out desperately for the other side, you begin to descend.

Pick a number from the *Random Number Table*.

If you have the silver Charm of Jnana the Wise, you may add 1 to this figure.
If your WILLPOWER total is greater than 10, you may add 2 to your total.

If your total is now *0–6*, turn to **274**.
If it is *7–12*, turn to **210**.

50

Before you can approach the main harbour gate, Shadakine war chariots thunder into the harbour area. The crowd scatters in terror, but the people cannot escape the rotating blades of the chariot wheels. Horrified, you watch as the Suhnese people are ruthlessly mown down by the Shadakine.

Suddenly one of the chariots swerves and hurtles towards you. You hear the insane laugh of the driver and as he draws closer you see that his eyes have no pupils.

You have barely a few seconds in which to act before the chariot is upon you.

If you wish to dive into the narrow street on your right, turn to **40**.

If you wish to stand and fight, turn to **155**.

51

You look down and notice that the Kazim Stone lies in the fire. Tanith stole it from your Backpack while you slept. (Delete this Special Item from your *Action Chart*.) You gaze into the Stone and see the haggard face of Mother Magri staring back at you. 'Now I have you, you young fool,' she hisses.

The glow of the fire grows more intense and bursts into renewed flame.

Turn to **102**.

52

You wake the following morning, drained and depressed. Your traumatic experience has caused you to lose 1 WILLPOWER point during your sleep.

'We must go on,' insists Shan, 'to make her sacrifice worthwhile.'

You know he is right, and wearily, you get to your feet and pull on your Backpack to continue your journey. 'We will reach the Azagad Gorge this afternoon if we set a good pace,' says Shan.

As the sun reaches its zenith, you notice how hot and humid the atmosphere has become. The plains of the Wilderwastes are now barren: a dry desert of ugly rocks and boulders stretches before you. You have many more days of travelling ahead of you and your food supplies are running low. The Azan river begins to narrow as you draw nearer to Lake Shenwu, the source of the river, lying beneath the Wall of Azakawa and the Shenwu Falls. Beyond that, lies the Azanam, home of the Lost Tribe of Lara.

Shan draws your attention to a wooden shack to the east. It is a strange sight so far from civilization.

If you wish to investigate, turn to **152**.

If you would rather continue your journey, turn to **227**.

53

You do not wish to arouse the fisherman's suspicions any further. For this reason, you are unable to bring about the necessary state of meditation that enables you to see into the future. Instead, you reach out with your senses in an effort to determine the fisherman's true nature. Totally unaware of your intentions, he continues to haggle over the price of the boat as you probe the invisible aura that surrounds him.

You sense that the one-eyed man means you no harm. He is the harbour watchman, a petty con-man who prowls round the harbour, spying on the illegal actions of smugglers and shady traders who he then forces to buy his silence. He is offering you half the true value of your boat. However, your power of Prophecy tells you that you might be glad of some money in the near future, and this may be your only chance of gaining some. You allow the watchman to cheat you.

The use of this Magical Power has cost you 1 WILLPOWER point.

Turn to **16**.

54

You head east, away from the line of the Azan River and into the 'Dragon's Teeth'. Further from the river, the limestone pinnacles are spaced at closer intervals, and you are forced to weave a zigzagging path between them. Though the ground is free from foliage, your progress is just as difficult as before, since it proves impossible to walk in a straight line for more than twenty paces before a stony column of huge, wind-worn rock blocks your path.

After an hour, you become lost in the dense maze of impassive rocks. The afternoon sun beats down mercilessly, as it slowly crosses the sky.

> If you have the power of Prophecy and wish to use it, turn to **278**.
> If you wish to turn left, turn to **184**.
> If you wish to turn right, turn to **228**.
> If you wish to continue straight ahead, turn to **238**.

55

You wait in silence, pondering the best course of action. A detachment of five Shadakine warriors, carrying crossbows, comes marching along the road; they halt to load their weapons only a few yards in front of you. If they should use their weapons against the brave knights on the bridge, the knights will have no hope of beating them off.

> If you possess the Magical Power of Enchantment and wish to use it to aid the beleaguered knights, turn to **70**.
> If you wish to attack the crossbowmen with your Wizard's Staff at long range, turn to **81**.

If you would prefer to make a surprise attack on the
crossbowmen, turn to **99**.

56

Still held above the heads of the crowd, you close your
eyes and try to concentrate. The noise and confusion
about you makes visualization very difficult and you
must lose 2 WILLPOWER points before the illusion is
complete. To your horror, you see that the two
Shadakine warriors have begun to hack a bloody
path through the mob towards you.

If you wish to continue with your spell of Enchantment, turn to **251**.
If you wish to break your trance and come to the
aid of the defenceless crowd, turn to **84**.

57

Instinctively Shan has thrown himself to the ground.
With your Staff thrust up high into the air you tear a
hole in one of the Quoku's wings; it shrieks with pain
before crashing to the ground. Your attack has cost
you 1 WILLPOWER point.

If you wish to attack the Quoku again, turn to **307**.
If you wish to escape, turn to **182**.

58

For three days, you head north towards the Chansi
Hills. During this time you regain 3 WILLPOWER points
and 6 ENDURANCE points. The dense forest provides
ample cover for your journey and you manage to
avoid the occasional Shadakine patrols quite easily.

You carry no provisions but Tanith is able to feed the

whole party. Demonstrating an uncanny mastery over animals, she is able to summon small birds down from the trees and rabbits from their burrows. Then after calling the mesmerized creatures to her, she coolly wrings their necks. Considering her part done, she insists that Shan should do the cooking and a disgruntled Shan agrees.

Coming at last to the forest's edge, where it borders on the Chansi Hills, you discover clumps of wild Laumspur growing along the river bank. If you have the Magical Power of Alchemy you may take some of the Laumspur and store it in your Herb Pouch. (Remember to mark this clump of Laumspur on your *Action Chart*.) Swallowing it will enable you to regain 4 ENDURANCE points. If you do not have the power of Alchemy and wish to regain 4 ENDURANCE points you must eat the Laumspur while it is fresh; you cannot take it with you.

You find a shallow ford crossing the Suhni River and stop to stare at the solemn hills ahead. 'We must go up into the hills to find the cave of Jnana,' says Tanith.

Suddenly Shan cries out, 'The enemy is upon us; look – the Najin are coming.' He points up at the sky.

Looking up, you see a cloud of ape-like beasts with grey skins and black, bat-like wings that propel them towards you at great speed. 'Do not fear,' Tanith says rushing forward.

'But Grey Star,' says Shan, 'these monsters are slaves of Shasarak, the Wytch-king. We are betrayed.'

The Najin swoop towards you, flying low along the line of the hills.

If you wish to attack the Najin, turn to **101**.

If you wish to wait for them to draw closer, turn to **126**.

59

You are hungry and must eat a Meal now or lose 3 ENDURANCE points. Finally, you lie down and quickly fall into a deep sleep. The night passes without incident, and your refreshing rest restores to you 1 WILLPOWER point and 2 ENDURANCE points. Then, you are woken by a strange sound.

Turn to **65**.

60

Without stopping for breath, you head up the next flight of stairs. You can hear Shan puffing and blowing behind you.

If you wish to take the right-hand stairway, turn to **45**.

(contd over)

If you wish to take the one on the left, turn to **80**.

61

Suddenly you look up, and for the first time you notice several squat shapes perched on top of the limestone columns nearby. 'Quoku,' whispers Shan. 'I thought they were a myth.'

The Quoku stare with unblinking, bulbous eyes. Like giant toads, their mottled, green skin is covered with ridges and warts, and their pale throats expand like bubbles as they emit their sonorous croaking call.

If you wish to try to slip past the Quoku without disturbing them, turn to **186**.

If you wish to attack the Quoku perched on the column nearest to you, turn to **111**.

If you wish to make a run for it, turn to **86**.

62

With heavy heart you greet the dawn. The old Shianti priest lies dead upon his pallet. After a short time the young girl who brought you food appears. 'Here – eat,' she says, poking another bowl of rice through the bars of the dungeon door.

'The old priest,' you say, pointing to his body, is dead.'

The girl glances towards the old man. 'I will tell Mother Magri. Perhaps she will want to steal his soul while it still lingers here,' she says, matter of factly. 'He was a silly priest. He deserved to die. But, perhaps my mistress can put him to some useful task.'

You and Shan stare at her, stunned at the coolness of

her tone and the casual way in which she dismisses the torment of a man's soul. She stares back, unconcerned; her face is a picture of childish innocence, and she seems unaware that she has said anything shocking.

If you wish to attempt a conversation with the girl, turn to **7**.

If not, turn to **36**.

63

'Fool!' she hisses. 'You have sealed your doom and I will not be a witness to it.'

She turns and leaves the circular chamber as it fills with a great number of Shadakine warriors. You are hopelessly outnumbered and the exit is blocked. Without your Staff you are powerless to resist the cruel Shadakine, who mercilessly cut you down where you stand.

Your life and your quest end here.

64

Your mind probes into the near future. Your Magical Power tells you that there is danger lurking in the alley-ways. You must continue along the narrow street to avoid it.

The use of this Magical Power has cost you 1 WILLPOWER point.

Turn to **195**.

65

You can hear a scuttling noise and the sound of a

66

heavy object being dragged along the ground.
Hurriedly you jump to your feet. By the pale light that
filters through the tunnel you crawled through, you
can see another tunnel leading out of the chamber.
The sound is coming from there.

You dash to the far wall, pressing your body close to
the tunnel entrance. You hope to be able to surprise
whoever, or whatever, is approaching. It is you, however, who is surprised. After a few seconds a huge
insect, at least three feet long and tugging laboriously
at the carcass of a dead reptile, clambers into the
chamber. Intent on its labour it does not notice you,
poised to strike.

If you are wearing the Salve of Yabari ointment,
turn to **72**.

If not, turn to **83**.

66

Even before you can lift your Staff, a crossbow bolt
flies past your head and plunges into the neck of the
Shadakine warrior, who falls with a surprised look on
his brutal face. The officer and his men hoot with
laughter at the plight of their own comrade.

While the first crossbowman reloads, the other looses
a bolt at you. The arrow burrows painfully into your
shoulder and you lose 3 ENDURANCE points. At the
expense of 1 WILLPOWER point you fire a blast at the
bowman; he falls dead. The first crossbowman has
now reloaded and you know that the odds on your
surviving another bolt are very slim. Even if you
manage to kill the crossbowman, you will have to
fight the officer, and already your shoulder is

beginning to stiffen. You are unlikely to be able to fight well in your present state.

You surrender to the Shadakine, throwing yourself at their mercy; a quality they seem rather short of.

Turn to **311**.

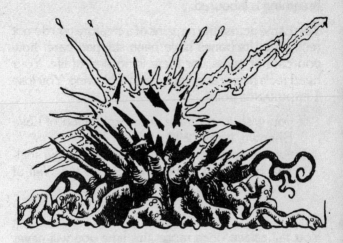

67

As you charge at her, she smiles bitterly. 'Fool,' she says; 'you have sealed your doom.'

Before you can reach her, she slips through the exit. You make to follow, but the room suddenly fills with Shadakine warriors. They pour into the room in overwhelming numbers through the trap door and the exit that Tanith has used.

The last sound you hear is the voice of Mother Magri ordering your death from within the safety of their ranks.

(contd over)

You have failed. Your life and your quest end here.

68

The waters of Lake Shenwu give off a foul stench. The heady vapours of this strange, yellow lake are thick and cloying. Your lungs feel tight and your breathing is laboured.

You came across the remains of a creature you do not recognize. Its bones have been stripped bare, how you cannot guess, for there is no sign of life. Your head feels heavy and your vision is blurring. You lose 1 ENDURANCE point.

If you wish to continue your exploration of Lake Shenwu, turn to **293**.

If you would prefer to climb the slope of the shallow basin and survey the base of the Wall of Azakawa, turn to **118**.

69

You fall asleep once more; this time you will never waken. Something dark and terrible leaps from the fire, and steals your life and soul.

You have failed in your quest; your adventure ends here.

70

You focus your thoughts in meditation, weaving a web of enchantment and attempting to influence the minds of the Shadakine warriors who are fighting on the bridge. Suddenly the Shadakine officer in command turns and sees the crossbowmen. His face contorts in fury. He barks a command and ten of his warriors turn and charge towards the crossbowmen, who look on in amazement. You have created the illusion that the crossbowmen are Knights of the White Mountain and, believing that the enemy are challenging their rear, the Shadakine have turned to attack this new threat. The use of this Magical Power has cost you 2 WILLPOWER points.

With a blood-curdling cry, the Shadakine warriors hurl themselves at the line of crossbowmen who instantly loose a volley of crossbow bolts, killing five of their fellow countrymen. The crossbowmen then throw down their weapons and flee along the road with the remainder of their outraged comrades chasing at their heels.

If you now wish to fire at the remaining Shadakine warriors on the bridge from the safety of your hiding place, turn to **88**.

If you wish to charge into the fray, turn to **156**.

71

The thief lies dead at your feet. After searching the body, you find your money plus another ten Nobles, which you may keep. You may also keep the thief's Dagger. (Don't forget to mark these items on your *Action Chart*.)

You leave the alley and return to the narrow street.

Turn to **195**.

72

The insect is unaware of your presence, and you keep very still. It continues to drag the reptile carcass across the room, finally it disappears through the narrow entrance of the other tunnel, and you breathe a sigh of relief. You seize this opportunity and scramble up the larger of the two exits and into another sloping tunnel.

Turn to **22**.

73

Using the remaining contents of the vial, you burn away the lock of the door. You no longer have any Ezeran acid and must discard the contaminated vial. (Delete Ezeran Acid from your *Action Chart*.)

The lock falls away and cautiously you push open the door to reveal another landing. You step on to the landing and face two more stairways, one leading to the left and one to the right.

If you have the power of Prophecy and wish to use it, turn to **92**. (Note down this section number first as you will need to return to it.)

If you wish to take the left-hand stairway, turn to **80**.

If you wish to take the right-hand stairway, turn to **45**.

74

You call encouragingly across to Shan who stares nervously over the edge of the precipice into the deep crevasse. 'Come on Shan, its easy. Quick now, there's no time to lose!'

Shan returns your gaze with a doubtful expression on his face. He shakes his head. 'I can't do it,' he says, weakly; 'I'll never make it across.'

You persuade him to throw his Backpack across to lighten his load, but he still lacks the nerve.

If you have a coil of Rope, turn to **194**.
If not, turn to **219**.

75

Following the road, you enter the forest. 'This road is busy by day,' Shan informs you. 'Many merchants and traders use it to reach the Port of Suhn. If we are to hide ourselves and rest, we must leave the road and venture deeper into the forest for safety.'

'The "pedlar" speaks the truth,' says Tanith, glaring haughtily at Shan, daring him with her eyes.

Shan turns purple with rage.

Turn to **3**.

76

Suddenly a knife flashes at your throat. Raising your

Staff, you unleash a blast of energy (costing you 1 WILLPOWER point) that narrowly misses the murderous cut-throat.

With a yelp of shocked surprise, the cut-throat turns tail and rushes back down the alley. You realize that while you remain here you are in danger. Retracing your steps, you watch him run into the narrow street and turn a corner. You follow the sound of his footsteps for a while, but soon you can hear nothing.

Turn to **195**.

77

You grab the Kazim Stone and throw open the door of the ante-chamber. Standing in the circular room, you see Tanith the young girl in the service of Mother Magri. 'Grey Star,' she says; 'at last I've found you.'

'Beware,' warns Shan. 'She is a Shadakine slave; she cannot be trusted.'

If you wish to attack the young girl, turn to **67**.
If you wish to question her, turn to **147**.

78

The dust storm continues to rage furiously; it gives no sign of abating. As darkness falls there seems to be no alternative other than to sleep here for the night, and hope that you will be able to continue your journey in the morning. You are hungry and must eat a Meal now or lose 3 ENDURANCE points. The night passes without incident and you regain 1 WILLPOWER and 2 ENDURANCE points.

The following morning you continue on your way,

following the banks of the Azan as it leads through the Wilderwastes and into the Azagad Gorge.

Turn to **29**.

79

Gently, you shake the sailor by the shoulder. 'Your pardon sir, are you feeling all right?' you ask.

The sailor opens his bleary eyes and frowns at you. 'Who wants to know?' he snarls.

And before you have spoken another word, the angry sailor jumps to his feet and takes a wild swing at you, upturning the table and spilling ale everywhere.

You are knocked off your feet, and hurled backwards to the floor. You must lose 1 ENDURANCE point. Dazed, you feel someone grab you by the collar and push you through the door. You tumble into the market square outside.

Turn to **157**.

80

With Shan at your side, you run to the top of the stairs. Above your head is a trap door. You throw it open and step into a circular room. There are two exits. Through the crack around the door opposite, you can see a faint, yellow glow.

If you wish to open this door, turn to **25**.
If you wish to take the other exit, turn to **41**.

81

Taking careful aim, you send a bolt of white lightning into the backs of the Shadakine crossbowmen, killing two outright at the expense of 2 WILLPOWER points.

The three remaining men look dazed and confused at this surprise attack. Shan can contain himself no longer and before you can prevent him he jumps to his feet. Brandishing his sword, he charges towards the remaining crossbowmen emitting a loud warbling cry. He is so close to them that you dare not risk another long-range assault for fear of killing him.

If you wish to follow Shan to protect him, turn to **99**.

If you would rather leave Shan to his fate, turn to **145**.

82

Tentatively you push open the door and enter a smoky room. The inn is filled with the sounds of contending voices, shouting drunkards and the laughter of serving girls. The customers are many and varied: merchants, seamen, fishermen and all sorts of travellers rub shoulders here.

If you have no money to buy a drink, or would prefer to save it, turn to **105**.

If you wish to buy a drink at the bar, turn to **339**.

83

The insect stops and lifts its head. Its antennae wave in the air, searching all around. Suddenly, it fixes its many-faceted eyes upon you and, before you can react, squirts a jet of brown fluid from a hollow horn on the centre of its head. You dodge to one side and the fluid misses you, hitting the floor. You look down at where it landed and see that it is eating into the stone. The insect opens its pincer-like jaws and drops the reptile corpse. Then, it scuttles back the way it came.

If you wish to attack the insect with your Wizard's Staff before it escapes, turn to **91**.

If you wish to chase after the creature, turn to **98**.

84

In desperation you raise your Wizard's Staff and unleash a crackling charge of energy that arcs above the heads of the crowd, and into the heart of the nearest Shadakine warrior. Your mind is in turmoil and you exert 3 WILLPOWER points on the attack due to its undisciplined state. The Shadakine warrior screams in pain and falls to the ground; blue smoke coils from the blackened wound in his chest.

With howls of delight, the crowd surges forward and falls upon the remaining Shadakine warrior as he lashes out desperately all around him.

If you wish to seize this opportunity to jump to the ground, turn to **196**.

If you would rather finish off the remaining Shadakine warrior, turn to **224**.

85

You wake the following morning feeling refreshed after a good night's sleep. Restore 1 WILLPOWER and 1 ENDURANCE point. Both Tanith and Shan have already risen and are waiting expectantly for you to lead the way.

Turn to **18**.

86

You repeat your prophecy to Shan and, taking his arm, you break into a trot, pulling him after you, though he seems to need little encouragement. Unfortunately your sudden movement attracts the attention of the Quoku, and a chorus of loud and rapid croaking fills the evening air.

The Wall of Azakawa is still many miles away and you pray that you will be able to out-distance the Quoku. Even if you should be able to reach the cliff face, you know no way of crossing beyond the wall into the Azanam. With a growing dread, you fear that your run will be in vain. Unless you can find somewhere to hide, or think of a swift way of scaling the cliff once you reach it, you will be caught. But despite your doubt, you keep running: you have no choice.

Turn to **266**.

87 – Illustration V

With a shudder, you step outside the pentacle and speak the sibilant words of the 'forbidden tome' known as the *Song of the Dead*. The ghost of the priest sighs and says, 'It is done. Take the Amulet from the body of my former life. It will serve as a charm against the evil dead.' You take the Amulet, which hangs by a silver chain around the dead priest's neck, and place it around your own. (Mark this Item as a Special Item on your *Action Chart*.)

All is silent. Slowly, the cell grows colder. The sound of distant moaning fills your ears, followed by a mournful wailing that chills the soul, which gradually rises in pitch and volume. The dead have come to claim their vengeance. The use of the power of Evocation has cost you 2 WILLPOWER points. A howling wind sweeps through the cell and the door bursts

V. Shadow forms are flowing out of the walls and floor

open. You turn and grab Shan's arm. He has stood, pale and rigid with fear throughout your exchange with the dead.

'Quickly,' you hiss. 'Come with me.' You run through the door and into the corridor outside. Shadow forms are flowing out of the walls and floor and everywhere spirit shapes fly in all directions. You turn to your right and see the horribly mutilated corpse of the jailer. Still clenched in his mortifying fist is a small Dagger. You may take this Item if you wish. (Remember to mark it on your *Action Chart* under the Weapons section.)

> If you wish to take the jailer's Keys and free the other prisoners on this level, turn to **125**.
>
> If you wish to take the left stairway without delay, turn to **137**.
>
> If you wish to take the right stairway, turn to **212**.

88

The bolt of force that arches through the air into the ranks of Shadakine warriors kills one of them at a cost to you of 2 WILLPOWER points. The knights gain ground at their opponents' expense due to the confusion of the Shadakine, who are now being attacked from the front and rear.

The distance over which you are fighting necessitates the use of a great deal of WILLPOWER, and you realize that you can only increase your effectiveness by moving closer to the Shadakine. An attack from the rear at this time would almost certainly turn the battle in your favour. With this in mind, you burst out of the undergrowth and charge into the battle with a fearsome yell. Shan, puffing and panting behind you, swings his sword feebly. The knights on the bridge give a rousing cheer as you appear, and the Shadakine are pushed back as their resistance begins to falter. And then you are upon them: you rain blows in all directions, throwing them into disorder and wounding a warrior at the cost of 1 WILLPOWER point.

Turn to **189**.

89

No matter how hard you try, you are unable to shake off the man who is following you. Soon he is joined by two Shadakine warriors. You have no alternative but to make a run for it.

Turn to **241**.

90

The camp-fire bursts into vivid flame, flaring high into the air. Wreathed in the lurid light is the figure of Mother Magri, who intones the words of a spell in a strange, guttural tongue.

'Grey Star,' says Tanith, 'beware!'

If you possess the power of Sorcery and wish to create a magical shield about yourself, turn to **139**.

If you wish to attack the figure of Mother Magri, shimmering above the fire, turn to **123**.

91

You bring your Staff down on the creature's unprotected rump. Its legs curl and crumple beneath it. At the cost of 1 WILLPOWER point, you kill the insect.

Close inspection reveals the insect to be a Cave Mantiz. The Cave Mantiz live in colonies below ground in much the same way as their cousins the ants. They burrow their nests from the stone by dissolving it with a potent acid that they store in their bodies. You have entered a Mantiz nest, and despite the perils therein, you are greatly encouraged. If you can find your way through the maze of Mantiz tunnels, you should be able to reach the surface above the Wall of Azakawa and enter the Azanam.

Your excitement is tinged with apprehension as you continue along a tunnel that is growing darker and darker. If you wish to expend 1 WILLPOWER point on lighting your Staff, you may: this light will last until you extinguish it without the use of any further WILLPOWER points. If you have a Torch and Tinderbox you may wish to use the Torch for light.

If you choose to proceed in darkness, turn to **122**.
If you prefer to light your way, turn to **141**.

92

Your power of Prophecy warns you that you must go left. The use of this power has cost you 1 WILLPOWER point.

Now return to the adventure number you have noted down.

93

The old Shianti priest is about to speak, when he gives a great gasp and dies in your arms. With tears in your eyes, you turn to Shan. 'He is dead,' you say sorrowfully.

The merchant hangs his head. 'Then we are doomed,' he groans.

You sit back, deep in thought. You are tired and quickly fall asleep.

Turn to **258**.

94

Staff held high, spraying magical fire from its tip, you charge the Shadakine with unflinching fury. Shan struggles in your wake.

The Shadakine warriors are thrown into disorder as they attempt to meet this new threat from the rear. Due to their confusion, the knights are able to press home their advantage, gaining ground on their opponents and raising your spirits with shouts of encouragement. You rain fearful blows in all directions with your Wizard's Staff. At the cost of 1

WILLPOWER point, you fell the nearest Shadakine warrior. Much to his surprise, Shan claims another.

Tanith now reappears armed with a loaded crossbow. Coolly, she aims it at the Shadakine officer. He falls to the ground dead, a crossbow bolt protruding from his neck.

Turn to **215**.

95

You examine the dungeon door, looking through the keyhole as you consult with Shan. Your Magical Power of Sorcery should enable you to produce sufficient energy to break down the door, but it is certain to require large amounts of WILLPOWER to exert a force great enough to burst the lock. You have no way of telling just how much WILLPOWER the spell will use, and once you have begun you will be committed to seeing it through to the end.

If you wish to force the door with the Magical Power of Sorcery, turn to **109**.

If you do not wish to use this power, or lack sufficient reserves of WILLPOWER, return to **172** and select another power.

96

In an instant your quick reflexes have saved you. You release a bolt of energy, costing 2 WILLPOWER points, that blasts the creature's head apart. The wound in your leg has lost you 2 ENDURANCE points and painfully you clamber to your feet, limping from the swarming death behind you. You reach a shaft that leads into the tunnel from above. You peer up it and see light. A way to the surface at last!

Clinging with trembling fingers to the nearly smooth sides of the shaft, you drag yourself up. Desperately, you haul your way up, kicking and stamping at the nightmare that advances from below. Using your last reserves of energy, you finally come to the top of the shaft. You are in a wide glade, surrounded by towering trees and dense foliage.

Turn to **146**.

97

Continuing on through the market square, you notice your pursuer stop to talk with two Shadakine warriors. He is pointing in your direction and gesturing excitedly.

If you wish to run from the market square, turn to **241**.

If you would rather try to lose yourself in the crowd, turn to **89**.

98

You follow the creature but it soon disappears from view. The tunnel curves slowly upwards and before long you are plunged into darkness once more. You stop running.

If you have a Torch and Tinderbox and wish to light the Torch, turn to **108**.

If you have your Wizard's Staff and wish to use it to cast a light, turn to **115**.

If you do not have either of these Items, or do not wish to use them, turn to **122**.

99

Leaping to your feet, you charge at the backs of the unsuspecting crossbowmen, your staff swinging and blazing a trail of magical fire. Shan attempts the same dramatic gesture, clumsily waving his sword, but fails to achieve the same effect.

Before the crossbowmen are able to release their arrows, you are upon them. Add 2 to your COMBAT SKILL owing to the surprise of your attack, plus a further 2, owing to Shan's presence. You must fight the crossbowmen as one enemy and to the death.

5 Shadakine Crossbowmen:
COMBAT SKILL 25   ENDURANCE 32

- If you win the combat, and wish to attack the Shadakine on the bridge, at long range, turn to **88**.
- If you win the combat and wish to charge the Shadakine, turn to **94**.

100

You have been prowling around the harbour for some time. So far all you have discovered are closed buildings, and shifty strangers passing in and out of the shadows, carrying mysterious loads.

You spot two soldiers patrolling the waterfront. Their heads are shaven save for a long plume of hair that flows from the centre of their scalps. They wear armour of black enamelled steel, decorated with gold designs, and carry lethal-looking scimitars at their sides. They are Shadakine warriors and they are shouting at you to remain where you are.

If you wish to run away from them, turn to **40**.
If you wish to obey the Shadakine, turn to **121**.

101 – *Illustration VI (overleaf)*

The first of the Najin is almost upon you when you unleash the power of the Wizard's Staff, killing one of the shrieking creatures in mid-air and scattering the others in all directions; you have used up 2 WILLPOWER points.

'No!' screams Tanith, running off into the barren hills. The Najin rally and gather around you, hovering. Yammering wildly, the first of the little creatures attacks you.

There are nine Najin and they attack one at a time, attempting to claw and bite you. If you have another weapon, you pass it to Shan who then adds 2 to your COMBAT SKILL. (Remember to delete this weapon from your *Action Chart*.)

Najin 1: COMBAT SKILL 10   ENDURANCE 10
Najin 2: COMBAT SKILL 9   ENDURANCE 10
Najin 3: COMBAT SKILL 10   ENDURANCE 10
Najin 4: COMBAT SKILL 7   ENDURANCE 9
Najin 5: COMBAT SKILL 8   ENDURANCE 10
Najin 6: COMBAT SKILL 10   ENDURANCE 12
Najin 7: COMBAT SKILL 9   ENDURANCE 9
Najin 8: COMBAT SKILL 11   ENDURANCE 9
Najin 9: COMBAT SKILL 10   ENDURANCE 9

If you are still alive after five rounds of combat, turn to **130**.

102

A flash of bright light ignites within the fire and seems to leap into your mind. You cry in pain, as if a

VI.   You unleash the power of the Wizard's staff, killing
      one of the shrieking creatures in mid-air

piece of your mind has been torn away. You lose 2 WILLPOWER points.

Stunned, you stagger backwards. The form of Mother Magri fades, and is replaced by an impenetrable darkness that hovers at the heart of the fire. Two blank eyeslits and a gaping mouth are all you see as the black shadow leaps towards you.

Turn to **149**.

103

Though you have beaten the Cave Mantiz the remaining horde of deadly insects overruns you and tears you to pieces where you stand.

Your life and your quest end here.

104

It soon becomes impossible to avoid the massed clusters of Yaku vines, and gingerly you step through, passing close to the spiky hearts of these deadly plants.

Your foot brushes a tendril. Instantly it writhes into life, coiling around your ankle with deceptive speed. You lose your balance and fall to the ground. Immediately you feel yourself being dragged towards the core of the Yaku plant, which lies only yards away.

If you wish to slash at the tendril that has knotted itself around your ankle, turn to **248**.
If you wish to unleash a bolt at the centre of the Yaku plant, turn to **179**.

105 – *Illustration VII*

You notice a spare seat and sit down. Also seated at the table are three others, one of whom may be able to help you locate the Lost Tribe of Lara. You try to decide with whom to attempt a conversation.

If you have the power of Prophecy, and wish to use it, turn to **313**.

If you wish to speak to the tattooed sailor who sits snoring beside you, turn to **79**.

If you would rather talk to the merchant, clad in a gaudy robe and furs, and laughing drunkenly to himself in the seat opposite, turn to **131**.

If you wish to speak to a hooded character, cloaked in black, sitting quietly in the shadows in the corner, turn to **209**.

106

You leave Jnana and the Chansi Hills. Tanith walks in accusing silence; she obviously holds you responsible for a foolish act. You wend your way back to the Suhni River and cross it once more. You have been walking for perhaps half an hour when suddenly three Shadakine warriors burst out of the forest – you have been ambushed!

Turn to **117**.

107

Shan stands motionless, his body frozen with fear. With one hand he holds his sword shakily aloft, while he covers his eyes with the other, peeping through the gaps between his fingers as the Quoku rushes towards him.

VII. Also seated at the table are a tattooed sailor, a
drunken merchant and a hooded character

At the cost of 2 WILLPOWER points, you punch a flaming hole through one of the Quoku's wings and it shrieks in pain. The injured beast is knocked awry; it veers sharply to the left and crashes to the ground.

If you wish to finish off the Quoku, turn to **307**.
If you would prefer to make another run for it, turn to **182**.

108

In the torchlight you can again see your surroundings. The ceiling of the tunnel is very low and you are forced to walk with your body bent over uncomfortably. At the end of the tunnel the exit widens, and standing a little straighter you continue on your way.

Turn to **135**.

109

You spend a great deal of time preparing yourself, pacing up and down the cell, while Shan looks on, mystified. When you feel you have reached the correct mental state, you focus your attention on the door. Your initial exertion of will has little effect and you gradually increase the strength of the spell. You have already used up 2 WILLPOWER points when the door begins to creak on its hinges, the thick wood warping. With a surge of effort you throw enough power at the door to use up 3 WILLPOWER points. The timbers snap and the joists squeal, but still the lock will not give. A last desperate attempt produces 4 WILLPOWER points of energy that splinters the door. A mighty noise echoes down the corridor as the door crashes to the ground. You have used 4 WILLPOWER points and lost 1 ENDURANCE point due to the prolonged strain.

You and Shan rush to the top of the steps and out into the corridor. Already, further down the passage to your right you can hear someone shouting. You recognize the voice of the jailer and the sound of his clanking keys.

If you wish to confront the jailer, turn to **243**.

If you wish to go in the opposite direction, turn to **333**.

110

Suddenly the rune begins to glow, burning its secret message into your mind. Its meaning gradually becomes clear. You hear the following words in your mind:

> *In Azanam the tribe of Lara dwell, no longer lost.*
> *Beyond the gorge of Azagad, when the 'Dragon's Teeth' are crossed.*

Turn to **190**.

111

You take aim and discharge a bolt of power straight at the top of the column. The Quoku lets out a long, chattering squeal of pain, but survives the force of the 2 WILLPOWER points of energy that you have exerted. Gouts of black blood flow from the ragged wound in its wing.

'Its hide must be tougher than armour to have survived that,' you gasp.

112

You are unnerved and make a dash for it; Shan is already running.

Turn to **266**.

112

You steer for the harbour and, as you near the stone quayside, you stand to furl the sail. You cut a dramatic figure: hair flowing in the wind; the reddening glow of the setting sun at your back, casting your shadow upon the shallow waters of the Sea of Dreams.

The harbour is very busy; crowds of people rush to and fro. Sailors and fishermen line the harbour wall, busily unloading their crafts in an effort to finish before nightfall. You notice a flurry of activity further along the quayside; by the time you reach it a small crowd has gathered, and you can hear the murmur of excited conversation. You throw up a rope and eager hands reach out to clutch the line, mooring the boat for you.

The crowd has grown and it is now obvious that you are the focus of their attention. You hear snatches of conversation: 'An Ancient One, an Ancient One from beyond the Sea of Dreams . . .' 'See you there? Surely a Shianti walks amongst us?' 'Saw him myself, came right out of the east, calm as you please!' 'God of legend, saviour of our people, hail, hail!'

Hands stretch out in greeting, while others try desperately to touch your robe, pushing and pulling, as more and more people struggle for a glimpse of your face. 'Who but a god could cross the Sea of Dreams.' 'Save us, Lord!' the crowd begins to shout.

'Destroy the evil Shadakine. Throw down the Wytch-king!'

You can feel the growing hysteria, and to your dismay you are lifted up on the shoulders of some of the crowd and carried in the direction of two armed soldiers, who are rushing towards you with their swords drawn.

'Destroy the Shadakine warriors, Lord!' someone shouts.

> If you wish to do as the crowd suggests, turn to **84**.
> If you wish to try to escape the crowd and the Shadakine warriors, and possess the Magical Power of Enchantment, turn to **56**.
> If you would rather try to escape without the aid of magic, turn to **28**.

113

You climb around the cave and head upwards. Gradually, the cliff face becomes sheer and smooth, and soon you can no longer find another handhold: the nearest crevice in the cliff face lies just out of reach. Your body is racked with fatigue and you barely have enough energy to continue.

> If you wish to reach for the crevice with an outstretched hand turn to **138**.
> If you wish to accept defeat at the Wall of the Azakawa, turn to **188**.

114

You concentrate the power of your mind and hurl the magical energy of Sorcery at the door. At first nothing happens, but eventually, after exerting 2 WILLPOWER points, the lock snaps and the door swings open.

You cross to the other side of the landing where stairways lead off to the left and right.

If you have the power of prophecy and wish to use it, turn to **92**. (Note down this section number first, as you will need to return to it.)

If you wish to take the left-hand stairway, turn to **80**.

If you would rather take the right-hand stairway, turn to **45**.

115

At the expense of 1 WILLPOWER point you cause your Staff to light. The light from the Staff will now last until you extinguish it – you will not need to expend more WILLPOWER points to keep it alight.

You continue along the tunnel, stooping because of the low ceiling. At last it widens slightly: you have come to the end of the tunnel.

Turn to **135**.

116

You gather up the power of your thought, forming a mental shield against the groping fingers of the Kazim Stone. A cloud of displeasure passes across Mother Magri's face. The magic of the Stone hovers at the edge of your senses; the explorative fingers probe your defence, searching for a weakness, a breach in the psychic wall. Your flesh prickles and creeps as the power of the Stone pries and pulls at your will, yet still you keep it at bay (at the cost of 1 WILLPOWER point). The old woman scowls, intent upon the glowing Stone.

The intensity of the stone increases and you must use another WILLPOWER point to match its strength. Mother Magri glares at you, her face twisted with frustration. She doubles the force of the Stone's power, her eyes straining and her breathing beginning to quicken.

If you wish to use another 2 WILLPOWER points to withstand this assault, turn to **150**.

If you would prefer to try to exert the influence of your will against your opponent from behind your shield of Sorcery, turn to **226**.

117

The Shadakine are spoiling for a fight, having tracked you for a day. Spitting war cries, their white eyes rolling, they charge towards you. In berserk fury the first of the Shadakine runs straight into the path of your staff and you despatch him easily at the cost of 1 WILLPOWER point. The events of the past few days have improved your battle skills immensely.

The two remaining Shadakine are more cautious than their dead comrade, circling and snarling, jabbing at you with their sword tips as if taunting a caged animal. You cannot evade and must fight them to the death.

2 Shadakine Warriors:
COMBAT SKILL 15   ENDURANCE 25

If you win, turn to **164**.

118

Standing at the foot of the towering cliffs, you look up. The cliffs are smooth and sheer; there seems no way of climbing them. The curling wisps of mist from Lake Shenwu swirl below and you move across the scree at the base of the Azakawa Wall, searching for a way up. Your head feels fuzzy and you lose 1 ENDURANCE point.

Suddenly you see a crack in the cliff a few feet above your head. It is a small niche, but is large enough to hide a man.

If you wish to investigate the crack in the cliff, turn to **268**.
If you wish to return to the Shenwu Falls and the area around Lake Shenwu, turn to **293**.

119

Without hesitation, Shan obeys. Bringing his sword up above his head, he bellows a cry and plunges it deep into the Yaku plant. The tendrils that hold you shudder, tighten, then suddenly, wilt, freeing you both as the plant writhes in the throes of death.

You have lost 2 ENDURANCE points in the struggle.

Shan has saved your life and you thank him through the pain of your bruised and battered ribs.

Turn to **128**.

120

You hurl yourself into the mass of fighting soldiers. At the cost of 1 WILLPOWER point, you throw down two Shadakine warriors. Shan disarms a third with a lucky blow.

The Shadakine warriors have become disordered by your attack, but you are still surrounded by four of them, who originally were commanded to guard the rear. You must fight them as one enemy and to the death. Shan adds 3 to your COMBAT SKILL for the duration of the combat.

Shadakine Rearguard:
COMBAT SKILL 25   ENDURANCE 30

If you are still alive after three rounds of combat, turn to **189**.

121

Two Shadakine warriors stand before you. 'What are you doing lurking around here?' asks one, prodding your chest with his fingers.

122

You fumble for some excuse, observing that the Shadakine's eyes are completely white – they have no pupils. You try to persuade the two soldiers that you are a local fisherman, but they are deeply suspicious of your story and appearance and arrest you on the spot.

If you wish to resist the arrest by attacking the Shadakine, turn to **265**.

If you do not want to reveal your powers and purpose at this time, turn to **300**.

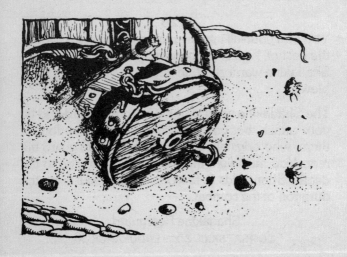

122

With great care you step forward into the darkness, following the tunnel by running your hand along the wall. After a few minutes the tunnel ends. You stumble blindly in the dark. Suddenly there is a terrible pain in your right leg as it is grabbed in a pincered grip. You are dragged to the floor and devoured silently by an enemy that you will never see.

Your life and your quest end here.

123

Fortunately you have your Staff with you. You lash out with it at Mother Magri, expending 1 WILLPOWER point. However, your Staff passes right through her: she is only an apparition, created by the power of her thought. She cackles hideously and begins to chant:

> *'Mundi Kleasá – Sorti Magri,*
> *Shasarak Shinto, Gordus Shando . . .'*

The apparition of Mother Magri dissolves, to be replaced by a sinister shadow, an impenetrable blackness at the heart of the raging fire. Two eyeslits and a gaping mouth are all you see as the shadow creature lunges towards you.

Turn to **149**.

124

You decide on Enchantment as your mode of escape: perhaps the jailer could be persuaded to open your cell door? A plan forms and you sink into a deep trance, weaving an elaborate illusion in your mind.

'Fire! Fire!' you shout, pounding on the door of your cell. Shan looks at you strangely, for there is no sign of any smoke. 'Jailer, open up before the whole place burns down!'

125

After a little encouragement, Shan is soon persuaded to join in the charade and begins rushing around madly, yelling and pounding his fists on the door.

Soon, the jailer comes limping down the corridor and stops outside your cell. 'I thought I could smell smoke,' he comments. He can see great plumes of fire raging in the middle of the dungeon and billowing smoke escaping under the door. He is completely fooled by your illusion and his rattling keys are soon in the lock. The door is thrown open and you and Shan bound up the steps and out into the corridor. The puzzled jailer is left peering into the cell, wondering why the flames of the fire give off no heat.

The use of this Magical Power has cost you 2 WILLPOWER points.

> If you wish to pounce on the jailer while he has his back to you, turn to **243**.
> If you would prefer to run to the right, turn to **23**.
> If you wish to turn left along the corridor, turn to **333**.

125

You snatch up the dead jailer's Keys and run along the corridor, unlocking each door as fast as you can. One by one, the doors are thrown open and prisoners pour into the corridor, rushing in all directions. If you decide to keep the Keys, mark them as a Special Item on your *Action Chart*.

> If you wish to go back along the corridor to take the left stairway, turn to **137**.
> If you wish to go back along the corridor to take the right stairway, turn to **212**.

If you wish to enter a narrow passageway at this
end of the corridor, turn to **333**.

126

The Najin land and encircle you. Their leader steps
forward, yammering and pointing to the hills ahead.
'They wish to lead us to Jnana,' says Tanith. 'He is
their master.'

'I do not like this, Grey Star,' says Shan. 'It is common
knowledge that these beasts are used by the Wytch-
king and the forces of Shadaki as spies and mes-
sengers. Surely this Jnana is a servant of the enemy?'

If you wish to follow the Najin, turn to **161**.
If you wish to leave the Chansi Hills, turn to **106**.

127

As the Shadakine warrior crumples and falls, the
excited mob roar their approval. They hail you as a
hero and crowd around you cheering. A new sound
floats on the harbour wind and the uproar subsides.
You can hear the clatter of pounding hooves and the
rumble of thundering wheels. A wave of panic ripples
through the crowd. 'The Wheels of Death!' someone
shouts.

Three war chariots, driven by whip-wielding Shadakine, hurtle into the harbour. The chariot wheels
have blades protruding from their hubs, and as the
Shadakine plough into the crowd, the blades scythe
down anyone in their path.

In the confused panic, you see a chance to escape
into a dark, narrow street.

If you wish to run towards the main entrance, turn
to **50**.

If you wish to run down the narrow street, turn to
40.

128

You and Shan huddle together. You are surrounded
by writhing tendrils, though, for the moment, they
seem reluctant to attack. 'If ever a garden needed
weeding . . .' murmurs Shan.

Somehow, you must get past the deadly Yaku. They
have you trapped. 'We need something to divert their
attention for a while,' you say thoughtfully.

'Don't look at me!' Shan replies, wide-eyed.

Despite your desperate plight, you cannot help
smiling. 'Of course not,' you answer, 'but perhaps
there is another way . . .'

If you possess the Magical Power of Elementalism
and wish to use this power to escape, turn to
181.

If you possess the Magical Power of Enchantment
and some Calacena mushrooms, and wish to
use this method of escape, turn to **206**.

If you do not have either of these Magical Powers,
or do not wish to use them, you may attempt to
fight your way out by turning to **12**.

129

You leave the fearful Stone where it lies and throw
open the door of the ante-chamber. Standing in the
circular room is Tanith, the young girl in the service of

Mother Magri. 'Grey Star,' she says. 'At last, I've found you.'

'Beware,' warns Shan, 'She is a Shadakine slave. She cannot be trusted.'

If you wish to attack the young girl, turn to **67**.
If you wish to question her, turn to **147**.

130

You are beginning to tire. Suddenly Tanith reappears, leading a wizened old man who is shouting angrily in a strange language. At his command the Najin cease to attack, flying up into the air and off into the distance as swiftly as they came. 'Fools!' curses the old man, dropping to his knees by the body of a dead Najin. 'My children, my eyes and ears,' he moans bitterly. 'They meant you no harm. I sent them out in greeting.'

'Jnana,' says Tanith, pleading. 'They did not know; they did not understand.'

'Why did you bring them here, Tanith?' asks the blind, old man.

'We seek the Lost Tribe of Lara,' you say, humbly.

'You seek your doom then,' Jnana replies. 'The way to the Azanam is fraught with peril. Go now, you are not welcome here.'

Turn to **106**.

131

You strike up a conversation with the red-faced merchant. His name is Shan Li, a trader familiar with all parts of the Shadakine empire and many strange lands beyond. Carefully, you steer the conversation to the subject of the Lost Tribe of Lara.

'Ah now,' begins the drunken merchant with some relish, 'the legend, eh? Well, there are many stories, and in my travels I have heard most of them. No word of the Laranese have I ever heard in the far north, the free kingdoms of the Lastlands, nor here in the Shadakine Empire. No indeed, the only story I ever heard that seemed authentic came to me in the city of Elzian where I was trading with the Magicians of Dessi. There I heard a story of the exile of the Lost Tribe to the cloud forests of the far south, that perilous place named the Azanam. Others, though, speak of the forested Shuri Mountains.'

In a very loud voice, the merchant begins relating one of the many stories he has heard about the Laranese. You notice that many people are turning to stare, muttering and whispering. Before you can attempt to quieten him, a hand grabs your shoulder. You and the merchant have been arrested by four burly Shadakine guards.

Turn to **300**.

As you point your Staff towards the bridge, Tanith rises, takes a running jump on to the back of a crossbowman and spoils his aim barely seconds before he releases a bolt intended for Shan. With the practised ease of a professional killer, she skilfully cuts the throat of the crossbowman with her knife.

Meanwhile, you unleash a fork of crackling energy,

which brings down a Shadakine warrior standing by the bridge, at the cost of 2 WILLPOWER points.

Turn to **203**.

133

Submissively you hand over your money pouch. With a mock bow, the cut-throat takes it, grinning fiendishly. 'And now a little silence from you, sir,' he sneers. He lunges at you with great speed. The cut-throat is trying to kill you and you must fight.

Cut-Throat: COMBAT SKILL 10   ENDURANCE 12

You may evade after 2 rounds of combat if you are still alive; turn to **27**.

If you would rather fight to the death, and you win the combat, turn to **71**.

134

'You are right, Tanith,' you say, 'we need counsel. But who is this Jnana, and can he be trusted?'

'He has no love of the Shadakine for, fearing the power of his wisdom, they blinded him many years ago in the ignorant belief that they could prevent his far sight by putting out his eyes. He sides with no one. He can be trusted. We must head for the Chansi Hills, which lie to the north of here. Come, follow me.'

Turn to **58**.

135

To your horror you see another insect, larger than the first, blocking the exit of the tunnel. You have entered a Cave Mantiz nest. The Cave Mantiz live in colonies below ground, burrowing their nest out of stone by dissolving rock with the potent acid stored in their bodies.

If you can find your way through this maze, you should be able to reach the surface above the Wall of Azakawa and enter the Azanam. But first you must deal with the creature that stands rearing before you. It is a soldier Mantiz and its clacking pincers and clawing, outsize forelimbs tell you that it does not intend to let you pass.

Turn to **197**.

136

Treading lightly, and with great caution, you move forward. You look all around, your eyes searching for an enemy lurking in the shadows, waiting to spring out at you from behind a rock or boulder.

Shan is trembling visibly now and moves to draw his sword, but you motion him to stay his hand lest the sound should alert some dangerous beast. Still you can see nothing, but the strange croaking call persists, increasing in frequency and echoing all around.

If you have the Magical Power of Prophecy and wish to use it to identify the nature of your danger, turn to **345**.

If you do not possess this power, or would prefer not to use it, turn to **61**.

137

With Shan the merchant hot on your heels, you dash up the stairs, which lead to a small landing. There are two exits. The left exit is blocked by a heavy wooden door. To the right is an open archway leading into a narrow corridor. In the distance, you can hear the sound of screams and falling masonry. The ground below your feet trembles.

'Which way?' asks Shan.

> If you have the Magical Power of Prophecy and wish to use it, turn to **92**. (Note down this section number first, as you will need to return to it afterwards.)
> If you wish to take the left exit, turn to **142**.
> If you would prefer to turn to the right, turn to **163**.

138

As you reach desperately for a handhold, your foot slips and you fall away from the cliff face. You plummet towards the ground, stomach churning and heart beating faster – but not for long. As you hit the stony ground, your body is broken, and you are killed instantly.

Your life and your quest end here.

139

You concentrate the power of your thought and, at the cost of 2 WILLPOWER points, a shimmering field of energy encircles you. The form of Mother Magri disappears from the heart of the fire to be replaced by a far sinister vision. A great shadow of impenetrable darkness appears in the flames of the fire. You see two blank eyeslits and a gaping mouth as the shadow creature lunges towards you.

Turn to **149**.

140 – *Illustration VIII*

The sun has begun to set. Far ahead of you, heading west, you sight a small group of fishing boats. You see growing numbers of these craft as you continue on your way, occasionally spotting larger seagoing vessels. Then your heart gives a leap of joy. You can make out the distant shape of a coastline and a harbour full of hundreds of fishing boats and sail-ships. In the orange glow of the setting sun, the domes and spires of a city point challengingly towards the sky. This is the Port of Suhn, the first city you have ever seen.

If you wish to enter the port before nightfall, turn to **112**.

If you wish to wait for darkness to descend, turn to **280**.

141

At the end of the sloping tunnel is an exit. You pass through and discover an even larger tunnel, curving away to the right and left. As you stand there, trying to decide which way to go, you hear the scrape of gigantic insect legs.

A large soldier Mantiz is scurrying towards you from the right of the tunnel, pincers snapping and large, outsize forelimbs clawing at the air.

Turn to **197**.

142

You push the heavy wooden door and give a cry of frustration: the door is locked.

If you have the jailer's Keys, turn to **286**.

VIII.   This is the Port of Suhn

If you wish to try to open the door through the use of Sorcery, turn to **159**.

If you wish to try to open the door through the use of Alchemy, turn to **170**.

If you wish to take the right-hand archway, turn to **163**.

143

You give a cry of pain. Your future screams agonizingly in your mind. 'Death! Death and Danger!'

With a great effort you try to locate the exact source of the danger but your senses only shout that it is all around, to the left and the right, above and below, in front and behind. In the darkness of your fear you understand one thing: you must keep moving, for it is the present that holds the greatest peril.

The use of this power has cost 1 WILLPOWER point and 1 ENDURANCE point, owing to the shock of the experience.

If you wish to explore the basin and the area around Lake Shenwu, turn to **68**.

If you would prefer to find a way to scale the cliffs, turn to **118**.

144

All day long you have weighed in your mind which of your Magical Powers may best aid your escape and, as night falls, you prepare to make a decision.

Turn to **172**.

145

The crossbowmen's expressions change to those of astonishment as the berserk merchant rushes towards them, red-faced and screaming comically in a strangled voice. Lunging ineptly with his sword, he engages the three crossbowmen with a series of eccentric strokes, none of which find a target.

If you wish to fire another long range attack at the warriors on the bridge from the safety of your hiding place, turn to **132**.

If you want to help Shan, turn to **99**.

If you would prefer to charge the Shadakine warriors on the bridge, turn to **169**.

146

Standing in the centre of the large clearing, hemmed in on all sides by giant Azawood trees and clumps of sprawling undergrowth, you stand and catch your breath. A look around the glade reveals a number of holes in the floor, entrances, no doubt, to similar shafts to the one you have left.

In a relentless tide, hundreds of Cave Mantiz pour out of these holes and stream towards you. Suddenly a pair of waving antennae appears in the entrance of a shaft close to where you stand.

> If you wish to fire a bolt from your Wizard's Staff into the shaft by your feet, turn to **158**.
> If you wish to dash straight into the undergrowth turn to **232**.

147

'Tanith,' you say, 'you serve Mother Magri. What do you intend to do?'

'I know where your Staff is hidden,' she replies. 'I can take you to it and help you to escape if you will take me with you. Decide quickly. There is great danger here and we have little time.' You hear the running feet of the Shadakine guards coming from the stairs below and the voice of Mother Magri, barking orders and cursing the Shadakine in an angry tone.

> If you agree to Tanith's request, turn to **221**.
> If you choose to ignore her words, turn to **63**.

148

Squinting in the dusky light, you see a webbed hand appear over the edge of the defile. Shan gives a groan of disbelief as the wounded Quoku heaves itself on to the ragged plain. Doggedly it moves towards you, dragging its tortured body, possessed of an inhuman vitality.

You haul Shan to his feet and point to the south. 'Look,' you say, 'we have nearly reached Lake Shenwu; one last effort now.' You pull Shan to his feet and stagger across the plain at a painfully slow pace. Relentlessly, the Quoku trails behind, slowly gaining on you.

With a cry of frustration, you see that your way ahead is blocked by a deep ravine that stretches nearly six feet across. The creature is not far behind you and you realize that there is not time enough to circle around the ravine. The Wall of Azakawa lies tantalizingly beyond reach.

If you wish to jump across the ravine, turn to **49**.

If you wish to stand and fight the Quoku, turn to **233**.

149 – *Illustration IX (overleaf)*

'A Kleasá!' Tanith screams, 'a Soul-eater!'

You must fight the Kleasá to the death. For every round of combat, subtract 1 WILLPOWER point and 2 ENDURANCE points from your total. If you have erected a magical shield of Sorcery, subtract 1 WILLPOWER point and 1 ENDURANCE point for every round of combat as the Kleasá tries to claw at your soul.

Kleasá: COMBAT SKILL 25   ENDURANCE 30

If you are still alive after four rounds of combat, turn to **165**.

150

The power of the Kazim Stone is overwhelming; it undermines your resistance, and prys into the corners of your mind; it disturbs the dust of your memories and trespasses upon the hidden chambers of your dreams.

IX.   'A Kleasa!' Tanith screams, 'A Soul-eater.'

Mother Magri's eyes widen with spiteful pleasure. You are powerless to prevent her intrusion into your mind. You try to blank your thoughts, searching for the safety of the Shianti way, the solace of meditation, but it is useless. The Kazim Stone is too strong.

'There now – I see it,' rasps Mother Magri, scrutinizing the vague shapes and shadows of the Stone. 'Something's there, some hidden purpose or grand design. Agh! It is protected. Some power hides it. More wizard's sorcery no doubt. Will this mist never part?'

The hours of your ordeal pass slowly. Mother Magri chants and intones every charm and spell in every language that she knows, but she cannot penetrate the curtain that enfolds your memory, shrouding that part of your mind that bears your quest. It must be Shianti enchantment bestowed, without your knowing, by the masters of the Isle of Lorn. However, Mother Magri does not relent, and you lose 4 WILLPOWER points and 2 ENDURANCE points. You feel the growing pull of insanity and a raging madness clamouring in your ears.

If your WILLPOWER total has now fallen to zero or lower, turn to **237**.

If your WILLPOWER points total is above zero, or you have the Magic Talisman of the Shianti, turn to **348**.

151

It should be possible for an alchemist to mix a potion of acid capable of destroying the metal lock of the cell door, though you will need the correct ingredients to make up the following formula:

Ezeran Acid Potion
1 part sulphur
1 part saltpetre
1 part Ezeran crystals
Mix over a gentle heat.

If you have the ingredients in your Herb Pouch and an empty vial to mix them in, turn to **297**.

If you do not have all these ingredients, you must select a different power to aid you in your escape; turn to **172**.

152

You make your way to the shack. It looks deserted. The door hangs half open and the windows are overgrown with an innocuous, yellow/brown weed called Ogosho, indigenous to this area. You hear a rustling sound coming from within.

If you wish to enter the shack, turn to **252**.

If you wish to use the element of surprise and burst in through the door, turn to **277**.

If you think Shan should investigate, turn to **302**.

153

As you close the door you hear the sound of running feet. Four Shadakine warriors are approaching. You turn the key in the lock. 'Hurry, Grey Star,' Shan calls. 'There is no time to lose.'

The Shadakine are beating at the door, shouting furiously for you to open it. Next, you hear the sound of heavy thumping as they try to force the door open.

If you have the power of Sorcery and wish to bar the door, turn to **185**.

If you do not have this power, or would prefer not to use it, turn to **198**.

154

You grit your teeth against the pain of your wound as the ferocious Cave Mantiz springs towards you, its barbed claws thirsting for your vulnerable flesh.

Cave Mantiz: COMBAT SKILL 15   ENDURANCE 18

You may evade this combat after one round by turning to **4**.

If you win the combat, turn to **103**.

155

It is a brave but futile act. You release a colossal beam of death at the Shadakine charioteer just as the horses trample you underfoot, crushing every bone in your body and killing you instantly.

You have failed in your quest.

156

With Tanith and Shan at your side, you look towards the battle on the bridge. The Knights of the White Mountain have killed many Shadakine warriors, but it looks as though this time *they* will be defeated.

'We must go to their aid,' you say. You approach the bridge, intending to attack the Shadakine from the rear. Tanith has disappeared, so with Shan following, you prepare to charge.

If you wish to attack the Shadakine officer in command, turn to **215**.

If you would prefer to attack the main Shadakine force, turn to **120**.

157

You are standing in the market square. It is bustling and full of life. Hundreds of stall owners are selling their wares by torchlight. You wander round the square, looking at the stalls and the items for sale there.

If you have the Magical Power of Alchemy, turn to **183**.

If you do not have this power, turn to **26**.

158

You fire down the shaft, using 1 WILLPOWER point. The enclosed space of the shaft transforms the energy beam into a fireball that hurtles into the tunnel below. Soon, the shaft is clogged with the charred remains of insects.

You limp into the tangled undergrowth, gasping with pain, due to the prolonged effort of running on your injured leg. The dense foliage and huge Azawood roots make for slow progress as you stumble through the brush. The Cave Mantiz have not given up their pursuit and swarm through the forest depths at an alarming speed. Thousands of enraged insects scuttle and scurry towards you. Your heart pounds and you fear that you cannot outrun them.

Turn to **232**.

159

Your power of Sorcery should enable you to burst the door open, but it will use up a great deal of WILLPOWER points to break the lock. You have no way of telling how many WILLPOWER points will be required, and once committed to this spell you will have to follow it through to the finish.

If you still wish to use Sorcery to open the door, turn to **114**.

If you have the power of Alchemy and would rather use that to open the door, turn to **170**.

If you wish to enter the open archway to the right, turn to **163**.

160

Gently you tip the liquid into the old man's mouth. After a short while, his eyes clear and a little colour returns to his cheeks. 'Thank you, brother,' he says. 'That was kindly done. I would return your kindness, but first I must sleep . . . sleep . . .'

You finish your food and sit back, deep in thought. You feel exhausted and fall into a deep sleep, chanting Shianti words of peace and meditation to calm your mind and free your thoughts.

Turn to **301**.

161

The hopping, fluttering Najin lead you into the stark, featureless hills. Eventually you come to a small cave entrance perched on a narrow ridge, overlooking a steep fall to the outlying hills below.

An old man sits cross-legged before the cave entrance, staring out across the heights with sightless eyes. Without lifting his head or looking in your direction, he speaks. 'Who comes? Who disturbs the solitude of Jnana?'

'It is I, Tanith,' she says. 'I bring Grey Star, a great wizard who dares to oppose the evil Wytch-king. He is in need of counsel.'

'I seek the Lost Tribe of Lara,' you say, 'for I have a quest and need their aid.'

The old man is silent for a while. 'You must go south to the great jungle of the Azanam. The way is fraught with danger, for you must pass through the great Azagad Gorge and the towers of stone known as the "Dragon's Teeth".'

'The Azagad Gorge is a vast canyon and the "Dragon's Teeth" are the great limestone pinnacles that stand throughout the gorge,' explains Shan. 'The Azagad Gorge ends at the great cliffs known as the Wall of Azakawa; the Shenwu Falls lie at their centre. Beyond and above the cliffs is the great cloud forest of the Azanam.'

'It is a strange land, full of weird and hostile beasts,' warns Jnana. 'You are unprepared for such a journey, but I will offer you such gifts as I have to aid you.'

He brings the following items from his cave and motions to you to take your choice.

A Silver Ring (a Special Item that Jnana claims will bring good luck)
Enough food for 5 meals
A Broadsword
2 potions of Laumspur (they each restore
   3 ENDURANCE points; may count as Backpack Items or Herb Pouch Items if you have the power of Alchemy)

A coil of Rope (Backpack Item)
Remember that your Backpack can hold a maximum of eight items.

Shan and Tanith are also given food, backpacks and weapons of their choice. Gratefully, you thank Jnana for his aid.

If you possess the Magical Power of Alchemy, turn to **193**.
If not, turn to **15**.

162

Taking careful aim, you fire at the chariot as it crosses the bridge. Because of the distance between you and your target the attack costs you 2 WILLPOWER points.

Your shot misses narrowly, falling just short of its target, but the fiery blast startles the team of black horses and causes the driver to lose his control over them.

Turn to **255**.

163

You run through the open archway and into a narrow passage that slopes downwards at a steep angle. As the passage becomes darker, a feeling of disquiet overcomes you.

Turn to **333**.

164

The dead bodies of the Shadakine lie at your feet. A thorough search reveals 10 Nobles and 2 Meals. Shan takes a sword from one of the bodies, smiling at you cheerfully. 'Souvenir,' he says in jest.

165

You may take the other Sword if you wish. (Remember to make the necessary adjustment to your *Action Chart*) before continuing on your journey towards the Azan river.

Turn to **39**.

165

The Kleasá seems to be growing stronger as it erodes your will. No matter how badly you damage the fabric of the creature you cannot alter the phantom's ability to feed on your spirit.

Suddenly the creature grows, wrapping its whole body around you, engulfing you in a terrible darkness. You lose 5 WILLPOWER points and 5 ENDURANCE points.

If you are still alive and your WILLPOWER score has now fallen to zero or less, turn to **177**.

If you are still alive and your WILLPOWER is above zero, turn to **192**.

166

You turn and stride purposefully towards the man who has been following you. Unfortunately, before you can reach him, he calls out to two Shadakine warriors and they advance towards you.

If you wish to try to escape from them, turn to **241**.

If you wish to confront the two Shadakine, turn to **11**.

167

'Run – both of you,' you shout to your companions.

Both Tanith and Shan ignore your command, bravely standing their ground by your side, though neither has a weapon. The chariot has now reached the bridge and it thunders on towards you.

If you wish to unleash a long-range attack at the chariot, turn to **162**.

If you wish to stand your ground and allow the chariot to draw closer, turn to **180**.

168

The sail lifts and you head out into the ever deepening waters. The Shadakine coast lies far to the west and you prepare for a long voyage. Two monotonous days and a night pass. During this time you must consume 2 Meals (cross these off your list of Backpack Items) and lose 1 ENDURANCE point due to fatigue, since you have had very little sleep, constantly ensuring that the ship maintains a steady course.

Turn to **140**.

169

Before you can approach the bridge, a crossbow-man, who has broken away from Shan's bungled attack, jumps into the foliage where you are hidden. He levels a loaded crossbow at your heart, grinning fiendishly. Suddenly his expression freezes in a grimace of pain. He falls forward and you see that Tanith's knife protrudes from his back. With a sigh of relief you bless her timely appearance.

'Quickly,' she snaps. 'Shan is in trouble. Help me.'

Turn to **203**.

170

If you have a prepared vial of Ezeran acid, turn to **73**.

If you do not have this potion, you can try to open the door with your Magical Power of Sorcery; turn to **159**.

If you would prefer to take the right-hand exit, turn to **163**.

171

A quick search of the body reveals 5 Nobles, which you may keep. You may also keep the guard's Sword if you wish. (Remember to mark these Items on your *Action Chart*.)

Now head for the other flights of stairs by turning to **137**.

172

Calmly you sift through these powers and the extent of your mastery of them to determine the most effective choice. You make your decision.

If you wish to try to escape with the aid of Sorcery, turn to **95**.

If you wish to use the power of Enchantment, turn to **124**.

If you would rather use Elementalism, turn to **271**.

If you wish to use the power of Alchemy, turn to **151**.

If you wish to use the power of Psychomancy, turn to **236**.

If you wish to use the power of Prophecy, turn to **211**.

If you would rather contact the spirit realm of the dead through the use of Evocation, turn to **250**.

173

'Fool!' she says, angrily. 'Now I must destroy you.' She points your Staff at you and unleashes a mighty blast that plunges directly into your heart. The burning bolt fells you instantly; you have become a victim of your own power.

Your life and your quest end here.

174

Shan is exhausted and you are obliged to help him along. The sky is full of Quoku, circling above you like expectant vultures. Ahead you can see the great Shenwu Falls that feed into Lake Shenwu, the source of the Azan River.

Shan whimpers in hoarse sobs. 'I can't go on . . . I can't go on . . .'

'You *must!*' you shout at him.

A few hundred yards further on, Shan collapses to

the ground, his body racked with fatigue. You look behind and see a familiar, yet amazing, sight . . .

Turn to **148**.

175 – *Illustration X*

'You have power young stranger,' murmurs Mother Magri. 'I sense some wizardry in you. How came this to be I wonder? Whom do you serve?'

If you do not resist the power of the Kazim Stone, your quest and its origin will be revealed to this servant of the Wytch-king.

If you have the power of Sorcery and wish to use it to destroy the Kazim Stone, turn to **191**.

If you have the power of Sorcery and wish to use it to try to shield your mind from the probing power of the Stone, turn to **116**.

If you would rather resist the power of the Stone with willpower, turn to **226**.

176

Panting for breath, your heart pounding against your ribs, you step on to the landing.

If you have the jailer's Keys and wish to lock the door behind you, turn to **153**.

If you would prefer to save time and continue immediately, turn to **60**.

177

You are too weak to resist and your soul is devoured by the dark phantom. You fall to the ground, a lifeless shell; you are another victim of the malice of Mother

X. 'I sense some wizardry in you,' murmurs Mother
Magri.

Magri and the dark servants of the Shadakine Empire.

Your life and your quest end here.

178

A young girl brings three bowls of rice, and lingers for a while to stare at you through the iron grille of the door. You thank the girl kindly for this simple act. 'Blessed is the giver, richer through the giving of a gift,' you say, according to the old Shianti custom. Startled, the young girl disappears.

You go over to the old man, who is obviously dying, and offer him some food. 'Twenty years,' he rants, gripping your arm. 'Twenty years I've been here, for no crime at all. Soon I will die.' Sadly, you learn that the old man was once a Shianti priest, a worshipper of the memory of your Shianti masters, imprisoned for his religion and for keeping alive the memory of the Shianti.

If you have some Laumspur and wish to ease the old man's suffering, turn to **160**.

If you do not have any Laumspur, or would rather keep it, turn to **93**.

179

Raising your Staff, you attack the Yaku. A fiery bolt burns into the heart of the plant and it releases its grip immediately. The attack has cost you 1 WILLPOWER point.

Suddenly Shan falls to the ground, emitting a startled cry; a snaking creeper is wrapped tightly around his legs.

If you wish to loose a bolt at the Yaku as it drags Shan towards its centre, turn to **285**.

If you wish to rush to Shan's side, turn to **240**.

180

You can see two Shadakine warriors standing in the chariot as it rumbles towards you. Just as you are about to hurl a beam of force at them, Tanith steps in front of you, directly in the chariot's path. She calls out in a shrill voice. *'Katta Chi!'*

To your surprise, the team of horses suddenly rears up, neighing in panic and confusion. 'I was taught the mastery of beasts long ago,' she cries, beaming with pride.

Turn to **255**.

181

With deep concentration you send your thoughts out to the elemental plane, unsure as to the kind of aid the elementals will send. The cost of this is 1 WILLPOWER point.

The clouds above your head darken, and with a smile you realize the nature of the help that has been sent to you. A sudden shower drenches the plants around you, their red hearts growing pale and their sharp barbs opening out into rows of tubules, drinking in the rarity of water from the sky.

As the plants lie limp and quiescent, you and Shan jump, with unchallenged ease, past the lethal Yaku and on towards your goal. As night begins to fall, Shan gives a sigh of relief: far off in the distance you catch your first glimpse of the Great Wall of Azakawa.

182–183

You break into a stumbling run, anxious to reach the boundary of the Azanam before nightfall.

Turn to **325**.

182

You decide to make another dash for it, and, turning in the direction of the Wall of Azakawa, you break into a run, Shan lagging at your heels.

Turn to **249**.

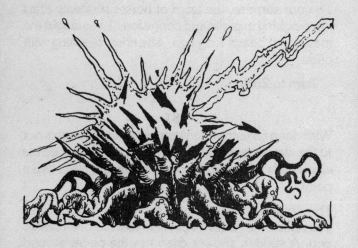

183

One stall in particular catches your eye. A sign reads:

MADAM TARLAS – HERBAL CURES & REMEDIES

APOTHECARY TO NOBLEMEN & KINGS

The stall is full of potions and salves and the dried leaves and roots of many different plants, some of great power and others of no use at all. Your trained eye notices several items for sale that could be of great use to you as an alchemist. They are:

1 jar of Ezeran crystals (which produce an acid capable of melting metal when combined with sulphur) .... Cost: 5 Nobles

A Pestle and Mortar (Backpack Item). Cost: 5 Nobles

1 bottle of Naptha (a volatile, inflammable liquid).
Cost: 2 Nobles

2 Vials of Laumspur (a healing potion that will restore 3 ENDURANCE points when swallowed).
Cost: 2 Nobles each

1 vial of Graveweed essence (a strong poison).
Cost: 1 Noble

1 vial of Alether (a potion that will increase COMBAT SKILL by 2 points when swallowed before an attack).
Cost: 2 Nobles

1 bundle of dried Azawood leaves (a base constituent that will charm up to 4 magical potions).
Cost: 5 Nobles

3 Tarama seeds (swallowing 1 seed permits a wizard to use his Wizard's Staff, or Magical Power, without losing any WILLPOWER points; they take up no room in your Herb Pouch or Backpack). Cost: 3 Nobles each

You may purchase any number of these Items. Items that do not fit in your Herb Pouch must be carried as extra Backpack Items. Remember to make the necessary adjustments to your *Action Chart*.

Turn to **26**.

184

You turn left and resume your journey. As you wind in and out of the pillars, you use the sun to guide you, keeping in a southerly direction.

As evening begins to fall, Shan sighs with relief. The columns have become less dense, and far ahead, you can see the Great Wall of Azakawa. It is a huge cliff face, many hundreds of feet high, stretching from east to west as far as the eye can see. Directly ahead of you, at the top of the sheer cliffs, you glimpse a huge cascading waterfall: the Shenwu Falls.

You move faster, anxious to reach the boundary of the Azanam before nightfall, and to leave this barren land of nightmarish scenery and strange inhabitants.

Turn to **325**.

185

'For pity's sake, what on Earth are you doing now?' questions Shan in a complaining tone.

'Hush,' you retort, closing your eyes to concentrate on preparing a holding spell to bar the door. At the cost of 1 WILLPOWER point, you create a magical barrier to bar the door. It will take the Shadakine guards some time before they will be able to break it open.

If you wish to take the left stairway that leads from the landing, turn to **80**.

If you would prefer to take the right stairway, turn to **253**.

186

Cautiously you creep away hoping that the Quoku will not notice you. Though you dare not look back, you hear the rustle of movement on the top of the nearest column where a very large Quoku is perched.

Turn to **86**.

187

Senseless with exhaustion, you are dragged forcibly from the chamber, down long flights of stairs and into the darkness of the dungeons of the Hall of Correction. Your senses rail against the ominous and overpowering feeling of oppression that seems imbued into the walls of the place. A tortuous scream fills the air, followed by the sound of brutal laughter. 'What was that?' you whisper, hoarsely.

'You'll find out soon enough,' one of the Shadakine replies. 'Jailer! Lock this one up!' A tattered cripple lurches towards you, a large bunch of keys rattling at his side.

'Here, Master Turnkey. Lock him up nice and safe now.'

The jailer limps forwards, a mad and joyous expression on his face. 'Marvellous, simply marvellous,' he giggles. 'Another guest. How wonderful to meet you.'

An iron-shod door is unlocked and you are thrown into a dark and foul-smelling pit. You fall headlong down a flight of steps and lose consciousness before coming to rest on the straw-covered floor.

If you have visited the Inn of the Laughing Moon, turn to **230**.

If not, turn to **261**.

188

Reluctantly you retrace your way back down the cliff, clawing and stretching for every precarious gap in the rock. Your descent proves tedious and tiring. At length, you reach the small cave and haul yourself inside.

Careful to make as little sound as possible, you explore the tiny cave.

Turn to **8**.

189

Suddenly you are confronted by the Shadakine officer. He gives a crazed yell before hurling himself at you.

The officer is a formidable opponent, and you can not safely evade combat without risking being cut down by this fanatic. You must fight him to the death. Since Shan is with you, add 3 points to your COMBAT SKILL for the duration of this combat.

Shadakine Officer:
COMBAT SKILL 25   ENDURANCE 26

If you win the combat, turn to **215**.

190

'We go south,' you say to Shan.

'Very well,' he replies. 'I only pray that I am not leading you on a fool's errand.'

'With you leading, what else could it be?' says Tanith under her breath, smiling sweetly at Shan. Within minutes, the two are trading curses and insults.

'We have no time for this,' you admonish them. 'Shan, lead the way.' Abashed, he obeys.

'At the heart of this forest,' he says, 'the Suhni River is joined by the Azan River. The Azan River will lead us all the way to the Azanam. We have a choice of two routes to the Azan. North of here is the Suhni River, which leads west, finally merging with the Azan. South lies the Great Suhn Road, which we left last night; it crosses the Azan further south. Which way Grey Star?'

Consult the map at the front of the book before making your decision.

If you wish to find the Azan River by travelling first north, and then west, following the Suhni River, turn to **38**.

If you would rather travel first south, and then west along the Great Suhn Road, turn to **21**.

191

Concentrating your will, you tap the raw energy of Sorcery from the astral plane, and form it into a ball of pure thought, holding it poised in your mind, ready to hurl into the Kazim Stone.

If you wish to draw 2 WILLPOWER points into your mind, turn to **323**.

If you wish to draw 3 WILLPOWER points into your mind, turn to **150**.

If you wish to draw 4 WILLPOWER points, turn to **320**.

(Remember to adjust your WILLPOWER total to its new value before turning to the appropriate section.)

192

You are smothered in an all-consuming darkness. Somewhere, seemingly far off, a muffled cry reaches your ears. It is Shan. 'Tanith, you must save him,' he cries. Then you hear Tanith's clear and brave voice for the last time . . .

Turn to **276**.

193

When you tell Jnana that you are versed in the arts of Alchemy, he offers you the following Items:

A Pestle and Mortar
A packet of Ezeran crystals
1 jar of Yabari ointment (a salve that will keep insects away and disguise the human scent)
4 Tarama seeds (swallowing 1 seed of this rare flower permits a wizard to use his Wizard's Staff, or Magical Power, without expending any WILLPOWER points; they take up no room in your Backpack or Herb Pouch).

You may take any of these items. Carry them in your Herb Pouch unless otherwise indicated. Remember to mark the Items you take on your *Action Chart*.

Turn to **15**.

194

Carefully you throw the Rope towards Shan but, overwhelmed by his fear, he is unable to catch it; you make three attempts before Shan grabs hold of it. You watch the injured Quoku come to a halt a short distance from Shan as the terrified merchant is trying to tie the Rope around his waist, with fumbling fingers. You wait, your nerves on edge, ready to pull Shan across the ravine, once he has secured the Rope. Still the Quoku comes no closer and before you can guess the reason, it is too late!

Turn to **269**.

195

The narrow street widens and grows lighter. The source of the light is the window of a grim, stone building at the end of the street, which opens on to the market square. Above the doorway of the building hangs a sign, which reads.:

INN OF THE LAUGHING MOON

You decide that you must try to find some information from the Suhnese inhabitants. Perhaps you can pick up some clues about the whereabouts of the Lost Tribe of Lara.

If you wish to try to gain this information in the market square, turn to **157**.

If you would rather enter the Inn of the Laughing Moon, turn to **82**.

196

You twist your body in the air and leap to the ground. The frenzied crowd have focused all their attention and hatred on the remaining Shadakine warrior, allowing you to lose yourself in the throng. Pushing and shoving, you battle through the press of bodies and try not to think about the warrior's ghastly fate at the hands of the bloodthirsty mob.

You are standing at the corner of a dark, narrow street that leads out of the harbour. The only other exit is the crowded main entrance, through which people are still pouring, attracted by the commotion.

If you wish to leave the harbour by the main entrance, turn to **50**.

If you wish to leave the harbour by the narrow street, turn to **40**.

197 – *Illustration XI*

The speed and ferocity of the soldier Mantiz is astonishing. The creature attacks. You cannot evade combat and must fight this deadly opponent to the death.

Soldier Mantiz: COMBAT SKILL 15   ENDURANCE 10

If you win the combat, turn to **213**.

198

The crack of timber makes you start, and you turn to see an axe smashing through the door. The Shadakine warriors are chopping down the door and it will not hold for long.

If you wish to run up the stairway that leads from the left of this landing, turn to **80**.

If you would prefer to take the stairway on the right, turn to **225**.

199

You are standing in a small dell. Ahead lies the Suhni River and beyond the river, a forest. 'Come,' says Tanith, 'there is a bridge nearby. We must cross the bridge to gain the safety of the forest before we can rest.'

'The witch speaks the truth,' comments Shan, returning the girl's icy glare contemptuously. Though you have barely rested, you continue onwards, coming at last to a wide road that crosses the Suhni River by means of a large, ornate bridge.

'It will not be long before the Shadakine come searching for us,' says Tanith. 'Have you a spell that would destroy this bridge and hinder their pursuit?'

XI.   The speed and ferocity of the soldier Mantiz is
astonishing

If you wish to destroy the bridge with the power of Elementalism, turn to **31**.

If you would prefer to create a barrier with the aid of the power of Sorcery, turn to **48**.

If you would rather conserve your energy, turn to **244**.

200

You enter the dark, narrow street. Tall warehouse buildings rise up on either side, casting deep pools of shadow that hide your passing. You have walked a short distance when you come to a crossroads. The right and left turnings lead into alley-ways, while the narrow street continues ahead.

If you wish to turn into the left alley-way, turn to **223**.

If you wish to turn into the right alley-way, turn to **76**.

If you would rather continue along the narrow street, turn to **195**.

201

When you waken, night is falling. Your rest has greatly refreshed you: restore 1 ENDURANCE point and 1 WILLPOWER point.

It is clear that you will have to use one of your Magical Powers if you are to escape the tortures of the Darkling Room. Carefully, you weigh in your mind which of your powers will best effect your escape.

Turn to **172**.

202

You stand up in the boat, close your eyes and with your hands raised you enter the required trance state with practised ease, chanting in the secret language of the elementals, and sending out the power of your thought to the elemental plane.

A few moments pass. The breeze begins to lift and the sail fills. You open your eyes and smile with satisfaction. All around are the fleeting forms of Wind Sprites, air elementals sent to hasten your voyage. Then a sudden gust of wind appears out of nowhere and the little boat lurches forward, throwing you to the deck; with a whoop of delight, a Gale Wraith has thrown itself into the taut sail and is propelling the boat forward with great force.

'I thank thee, powers of the air,' you shout with joyous courtesy, struggling to sit up in the boat to steer her on the right course. The spell has been successful and required little power. Deduct 1 point from your WILLPOWER total.

Turn to **140**.

203

She swiftly retrieves her knife and wipes the blood on the dead man's tunic before pouncing on the two soldiers that threaten Shan.

In seconds, you and Tanith have engaged the two remaining crossbowmen, much to the relief of Shan, whose eyes are now bulging with fear. The Shadakine offer no surrender, and you must fight them to the death. Since you have the aid of Tanith and Shan, you may add 4 points to your COMBAT SKILL for the duration of the fight.

2 Shadakine Crossbowmen:
COMBAT SKILL 15   ENDURANCE 18

If you win, turn to **156**.

204

At the cost of 2 WILLPOWER points, you lash out at the tendril that holds Shan. The energy beam slices through the creeper. It withers instantly and releases him.

In the time that it has taken you to free Shan, two more creepers have crawled towards you. One is curled around your right leg, the other grips your left ankle. The creepers must belong to different Yaku plants, for you can feel yourself being pulled in two directions. Once more you are dragged to the ground and the pain becomes unbearable as your body is stretched apart.

As you are forcibly dragged to the ground you may fire at the heart of the nearest Yaku plant, which is only a Staff's length away, by turning to **329**.

If you would prefer to attack the Yaku vine holding your right leg, turn to **279**.

If you wish to attack the Yaku vine on your left leg, turn to **304**.

205

You push a key into the lock and turn it: it is the wrong key. Dismayed, you try another.

Suddenly, the door is pulled open from the other side. A Shadakine warrior stands in the doorway. With an astonished cry, he draws his sword and attacks.

Add 5 points to your COMBAT SKILL for the duration of this fight owing to the advantage of surprise and Shan's help.

Shadakine Warrior:
COMBAT SKILL 11   ENDURANCE 15

> If you wish to evade this combat (which you may do at any time by fleeing down the right-hand exit), turn to **163**.
>
> If you win the fight, turn to **176**.

206

You swallow the mushrooms and wait for the effect to take a hold. The pink fungi enables you to communicate with the vicious plants, sending out waves of passivity. Soon the plants become dull and docile and you are able to tread a safe path through them.

The light is fading when at last you come within sight of the Great Wall of Azakawa.

Turn to **325**.

207

Your Torch sputters and goes out, plunging you into darkness. There is no time to make another light and you swing blindly at your enemies, who soon overwhelm you.

Your life and your quest end here.

208

As you emerge from the forest you see a detachment of five Shadakine warriors, carrying crossbows, marching along the road towards you. You are now trapped between them and the battle on the bridge.

> If you wish to attack the crossbowmen with your Wizard's Staff, at long range, turn to **81**.
> If you would prefer to charge the crossbowmen, using the element of surprise to full advantage, turn to **99**.

209

You speak to the man shrouded in shadow, noting the wooden, fish-shaped amulet hung around his neck. This is the symbol of the silent order of 'Redeemers', a religious sect persecuted throughout the Shadakine Empire, though their purposes remain a mystery.

Instead of replying, the black-robed pilgrim puts a finger to his lips and hands you two Items: a vial, containing a Pink Liquid, and a Medallion, inscribed with a rune. If you wish to keep these Items, mark the vial of Pink Liquid as a Backpack Item and the Medallion as a Special Item (worn around your neck) on your *Action Chart*.

Before you can examine these Items more closely, four Shadakine warriors burst into the inn. They seem to be looking for someone. Without a word, the 'Redeemer' leaves.
Suddenly, a mug of ale is placed in front of you. The affable merchant sitting opposite has bought you a drink; he is shouting a happy greeting to you and asking your name.

> If you wish to accept the drink, turn to **131**.
> If you would rather leave the inn, turn to **157**.

210

You reach the other side but stagger and fall, rolling over and over upon the dusty plain. You are shaken and bruised by the fall: lose 2 ENDURANCE points.

Turn to **74**.

211

Focusing your mind, you reach out into the future, expending 1 WILLPOWER point. The way is not clear, but repeatedly you are shown a vision of the dead Shianti priest. You are being urged to raise the old priest's spirit.

If you wish to do this, turn to **250**.

If you have already attempted the spell of Evocation or wish to ignore the vision, turn to **172** and select another Magical Power.

212

You have entered a small room. A Shadakine guard is sleeping in a chair, his back turned towards you.

If you wish to attack the Shadakine guard, turn to **309**.

If you prefer to leave the room as quietly as possible and take the other stairway, turn to **137**.

213

You must move quickly now. You enter an unguarded tunnel that lies to the left and break into a run. At length you come to the two exits: one slopes upwards, the other, downwards.

If you wish to enter the passage sloping upwards, turn to **267**.

214

If you wish to enter the passage sloping downwards, turn to **272**.

If you would prefer to return the way you came, turn to **284**.

214

The lock clicks open. 'Thank the gods,' you breath.

'Thank the jailer,' quips Shan, wiping the sweat from his brow. You throw open the door and discover another landing. There are two stairways, one leading to the left and the other to the right.

If you have the power of Prophecy and wish to use it, turn to **92**. (Note down this section number first as you will need to return to it.)

If you wish to take the left stairway, turn to **176**.

If you would prefer to take the right stairway, turn to **45**.

As the Shadakine officer dies, the Knights of the White Mountain give a victorious cheer and charge forwards. The Shadakine that remain continue to fight but eventually falter and retreat into small groups. With their numbers divided into small pockets of resistance, the knights are quickly able to overcome them, demonstrating their superior fighting skills in one to one combat. The Shadakine warriors fight to the last man and you expend another WILLPOWER point before the battle is over.

As soon as the fighting is over, the unarmed man jumps down from the wagon on to the bridge. 'My thanks, stranger. A timely arrival indeed,' he says, smiling broadly.

His name is Madin Rendalim, a Durenese herb warden, famous throughout the Lastlands of the far north for his knowledge and skill in the healing arts. He is journeying through the provinces of the Shadakine Empire seeking the Druse tree, and the clear, sticky resin beneath its bark – the only known cure for the terrible Red Death plague.

'I had found the Druse tree growing some distance from here, in the Forest of Fernmost at the foot of the Kashima Mountains. I was returning to Port Suhn to journey back to my home in Hammerdal when these ill-mannered Shadakine brutes refused to let us pass. They have closed the roads around Suhn it seems, searching for some fugitives or outlaws.'

As a sign of his gratitude he offers you the following items:

1 potion of Randalim's Elixir (restores 6 ENDURANCE points)

Enough food for 5 Meals

A Pestle and Mortar (Backpack Item)

3 Tarama flower seeds (1 seed permits the use of a Magical Power or Wizard's Staff without the loss of any WILLPOWER points)

Sealed pouch of Calacena mushrooms (the spores of these mushrooms may enhance the illusions of those using the power of Enchantment).

You may take any of these items. Carry them in your Herb Pouch unless otherwise indicated, or unless you have no Herb Pouch, in which case carry them in your Backpack. Remember to mark the items on your *Action Chart*.

When you have made your choice, he offers Shan and Tanith a selection of gifts. At last, you bid the herb warden and his brave bodyguard farewell, requesting that they mention your encounter to no one.

Turn to **2**.

216

Desperately, you twist towards the plant. The Dagger misses the centre of the Yaku plant by an inch but there is no time for a second blow. You are wrenched into the crimson heart of the Yaku.

The pain of a hundred barbs, plunging into your face soon fades as you fall into the oblivion of death.

You have failed in your quest.

217

Cautiously, you begin to fish for information. The shrewd eyes of the innkeeper narrow and he leans towards you, speaking in a low voice. 'It it's information you're after, you'd best remember that these are dangerous times,' he says, 'and dangerous talk costs lives they say, if you take my meaning sir,' he adds, stretching his upturned palm towards you.

You drop one Noble into his hand, but he only shakes his head saying, 'And life doesn't come cheap, now, does it sir?'

The innkeeper only closes his hand when you have given him another four Nobles. (Remember to cross these off your *Action Chart*.) 'Now then young master, what was it exactly that you wanted to know?' Anxiously, you enquire after the legend of the Lost Tribe of Lara.

'The Lost Tribe!' he exclaims, incredulously. With a frightened expression, the innkeeper stands back. 'Never been outside Suhn in all my life,' he splutters, 'and that's forbidden talk, against Shadakine law. You'd best try them over there,' he says, pointing to a nearby table. 'they're travellers throughout these lands.' The innkeeper pockets your money and dashes away to another part of the bar before you can protest.

Turn to **105**.

218

On the afternoon of the third day you have reached the point where the Azan River joins the Suhni. Shan is a good guide; he has read the trail well and you have made good progress.

'A few miles south of here lies the Village of Iwo,' says

Shan. 'There the great Suhn Road crosses the Azan River, but we must be on our guard as we approach the bridge.'

Turn to **39**.

219

Before you can react, Shan is being enclosed in the deathly embrace of the venomous Quoku, its wings obscuring him from sight and sealing his inevitable doom. You shudder with revulsion and look away as a wave of nausea rises in your throat.

Hurriedly you take up Shan's backpack and move on to Lake Shenwu. You dare not look back.

Turn to **294**.

220

In denying the dead, your soul is forfeit. Your spirit is wrenched from your body and hurled into the abyss to suffer eternal torment at the hands of the masters of darkness.

Your quest is over, but your torment continues – forever!

221

'Very well,' you say, 'lead on.'

Tanith gives a sigh of relief and points towards the ante-chamber of Mother Magri. 'This way,' she says, running into the room. With Shan muttering about death and destruction, betrayal and butchery, you follow her.

'*Casas Indu*,' she calls, and a hidden door slides open, revealing a dark space behind. 'It's a secret passage,' she explains. 'Here is your Staff and Backpack.' She takes a torch from the wall and its light reveals a small compartment, roughly hewn from stone, and a sloping passage heading downwards. You take the Backpack and Staff from their hiding place and turn to Tanith. 'What now?' you ask.

'Down the passage – hurry!' she replies. You and Shan run down the passage. Tanith follows swiftly. '*Casas Sendra*,' she intones and the secret door slides shut.

If you have the Kazim Stone and there is room in your Backpack, you may place it there for safekeeping. Remember to mark it as a Special Item on your *Action Chart*.

Turn to **292**.

222

You turn left, following the broad curve of the tunnel as it veers right. As you turn the bend you see a large soldier Mantiz up ahead. It is larger than the worker Mantiz that you saw earlier. Its forelegs are oversized claws and the upper segment of its body and its head rises vertically above its abdomen.

The soldier Mantiz is guarding an exit off to the right of the curving tunnel in which you stand. Attracted by your light, the Mantiz turns its bulbous eyes towards you and begins to snap its pincers in agitation.

If you wish to attack the soldier Mantiz at long range with your Wizard's Staff, turn to **239**.

If you wish to charge the soldier Mantiz, turn to **246**.

If you would prefer to head back the way you came, turn to **260**.

223

As you turn into the alley-way, the pungent smell of rotting garbage fills your nostrils. Rats feed in the gutters and the stink from the open sewer is overpowering. However, for the moment, you seem relatively safe. Now you must seek out some information on the possible whereabouts of the Lost Tribe of Lara. You must also try to keep your motives secret from the local Suhnese.

If you wish to seek this information in the alley, turn to **34**.

If you would prefer to head back to the narrow street, turn to **195**.

224 – *Illustration XII (overleaf)*

'Death to the Shadakine!' you scream, caught up in the berserk fury of the mob. With a triumphant cry, the crowd deposits you on the ground and then withdraws to form a circle around you and the warrior. The Shadakine stands sweating and panting before you; his eyes dart wildly in every direction but he sees no escape. As the jeering crowd hurls insults and taunts at the trapped soldier, you notice that the shaven-headed warrior's eyes are totally white, completely lacking pupils. Resolutely, he steps forward, sword and teeth bared, snarling his defiance. 'To the death then, boy,' he spits.

You cannot avoid the combat owing to the circle of people around you and must fight the Shadakine to the death.

Shadakine Warrior:
COMBAT SKILL 13   ENDURANCE 20

If you win, turn to **127**.

225

You have run half-way up the flight of stairs when the door at the top is thrown open by a Shadakine guard. The Shadakine behind draw closer and the guard at the top calls to the warriors from the guard room you were running towards. You are trapped.

Your last memory is of Shan's resigned stare as he succumbs to death at the hands of the Shadakine.

Your life and your quest end here.

XII. The Shadakine steps forward snarling his defiance

226

You enter into a duel of wills with the power of the Stone. The yellow glow of the Kazim Stone flares brighter and brighter, its burning fingers tearing at your mind. Beads of perspiration appear on your forehead as you exert your powers of concentration.

The combined WILLPOWER scores of Mother Magri and the Kazim Stone are 50. Add together your current WILLPOWER and COMBAT SKILL scores and subtract this total from 50.

If your final score is 15 or more, turn to **295**.
If your score is 14 or less, turn to **320**.

227

You press on, keeping close to the line of the river, and very soon you enter the Azagad Gorge. The hot sun burns down fiercely on the arid surface of the canyon floor, and the distant horizon is distorted by the haze of shimmering heat.

Turn to **29**.

228

You choose to go right and find it easier to maintain a constant direction. Gradually the towers of the 'Dragon's Teeth' become less dense. Soon the 'Dragon's Teeth' have disappeared altogether and you realize that the Wall of Azakawa does not lie ahead as it should. Shan stops and looks around the dusty plain. He groans as he sights the Azan River lying way off to the west.

'We've been heading north . . . We're back in the Wilderwastes!' he moans, slapping his forehead with his hand.

If you wish to head west, pick up the Azan River and head back into the Azagad Gorge, by your original route, turn to **328**.

If you wish to retrace your steps, turn to **6**.

229

A bolt of energy slices into the Yaku plant. Its tendrils tense, leaping into the air before falling lifelessly to the ground. Your attack has cost you 2 WILLPOWER points.

To your relief, you see that Shan has managed to free himself from the grip of the other Yaku plant.

If you wish, at long range, to attack another Yaku plant threatening Shan, turn to **5**.

If you would prefer to attack the cluster of tendrils slithering towards you, turn to **30**.

230

When you waken, your head aches and your vision is blurred. Realization of your terrible plight comes flooding back and you lift your head to look around. In the far corner sits the now sober and miserable figure of Shan Li, the merchant from the Inn of the Laughing Moon.

'So they got you too, friend,' says Shan Li, wryly.

Turn to **291**.

231

Owing to the speed of its approach and the steep angle of its attack, you are unable to let off a long-range blast at the Quoku. Bringing its back legs forward and using its body and outstretched wings as a wind-break the creature comes to an abrupt halt and lands smoothly. It has barely touched the ground, a few feet away, when it leaps towards you, limbs spread-eagled.

There are strange suckers on the tips of its fingers and toes and its warty skin oozes with a glistening poison. The creature is trying to engulf you in the folds of its wings in a poisonous and fatal embrace.

You must avoid contact with the creature's poisonous skin at all costs. Subtract 2 points from your COMBAT SKILL for the duration of the combat, because of the defensive nature of your tactics.

Quoku: COMBAT SKILL 12   ENDURANCE 30

If you win the combat, turn to **256**.

232

You are forced to a sudden halt, for the way ahead is blocked by a fallen tree. You turn and see a large soldier Mantiz rushing towards you and you gasp in frenzied desperation. You are trapped! Wounded and bloody you prepare to defer yet another attack, fear gripping your heart with an icy chill.

Turn to **154**.

233 – *Illustration XIII (overleaf)*

Standing your ground, you wait as the Quoku draws near, bracing yourself against attack. It stops a few yards away, regarding you with a baleful expression.

Suddenly, and without warning, the Quoku opens its mouth and grabs at Shan with a long proboscis-like tongue that wraps tightly around his arms and chest.

XIII.   Shan is dragged towards the venemous mouth of
the Quoku

Shan screams with fear and revulsion as he is dragged towards the venomous mouth of the Quoku. You have seconds in which to act.

Turn to **337**.

234

Taking the right turn, you are immediately stopped in your tracks by a terrifying sight. A large soldier Mantiz is running towards you, pincers snapping and large, oversize forelimbs clawing at the air.

Turn to **197**.

235

You press your fingertips against each of the keys, maintaining a vision of the door lock in your mind. One key feels right; you insert it into the lock and turn. The cost of this spell is 1 WILLPOWER point.

Turn to **214**.

236

Pressing your hand to the cell wall, you reach out with the power of your thought and search for guidance. You hear the moaning cries of the dead; the suffering torment of tortured souls that have passed through this place assails your mind. You hear voices chanting. 'Call the priest; call the priest.'

The cost of this Magical Power is 1 WILLPOWER point.

Now return to **172** and select a power to aid you in your escape.

237

Something snaps. A keystone in your brain crumbles, bringing the temple of your mind to the ground in shattered fragments: the Kazim Stone has destroyed your mind.

You live the rest of your life, a raving madman, wandering the countryside, wielding a Staff you cannot use, and pursuing a quest you can never achieve.

You have failed in your quest.

238

You walk ahead, still unsure of the correct direction. You feel as if you are wandering aimlessly around the sheer crags of rock, with their crowns of stony spires that give no clues to your whereabouts. An hour passes before a familiar sound greets your ears. It is the faint murmur of the waters of the Azan River. You spot a Yaku plant, and then another, then Shan gives a snort of disgust. 'That rock over there,' he says, indicating a large overhanging shelf; 'I recognize it. On the other side of that rock is the river bank. We're back where we started!'

Dismayed, you realize that he is right. This is the place where you first left the Azan River to avoid the Yaku plants.

> If you wish to leave the bank of the river once more and head east, back towards the 'Dragon's Teeth', before turning south, turn to **303**.
> If you would prefer to give up and take your chances with the thick undergrowth of Yaku plants along the river's edge, turn to **104**.

239

You raise your staff and loose a bolt of white fire at the insect. Your aim is true and the bolt sears into the head of the soldier Mantiz. The insect crumples and falls dead to the ground. The attack has cost you 2 WILLPOWER points.

Carefully, you advance and step over the smoking body of the soldier Mantiz. You enter the passage that it was guarding and soon come to two exits, one sloping downwards, the other sloping upwards.

If you wish to enter the upward-sloping passage, turn to **267**.

If you wish to enter the downward-sloping passage, turn to **272**.

If you wish to return the way you came, turn to **284**.

240

You run towards Shan. Quickly you realize that you will probably not reach him in time to save his life. You have no choice but to try to free him the quickest way you can.

Turn to **204**.

241 – *Illustration XIV (overleaf)*

You turn into a street leading from the square and break into a run. Behind, you hear the cry of a Shadakine, ordering you to halt.

You have turned into a busy high street, crowded with people, and try as you may you cannot clear a way through them. Suddenly the crowd scatters, diving for cover. Twenty yards ahead stand three

XIV.   Ahead stand three Shadakine warriors with
weapons loaded

Shadakine warriors, an officer and two crossbowmen with weapons loaded and aimed at your heart.

'Halt, or you're dead!' shouts the Shadakine officer, savagely.

If you wish to obey his order, turn to **300**.
If you want to attack them, turn to **66**.
If you would rather turn and try to make a break for it, turn to **20**.

242

The stones are very slippery and the river is wide at this point. You will need all your powers of concentration to prevent yourself falling into the foul water.

Add together your current ENDURANCE and WILLPOWER scores.

If your total is 20 or more, turn to **341**.
If your total is 19 or less, turn to **316**.

243

Without warning you attack the jailer who, despite his frail appearance, responds to your attack with savage blows. Owing to Shan's assistance and the element of surprise, you may add 4 points to your COMBAT SKILL for the duration of this fight. You cannot evade and must fight to the death.

Jailor: COMBAT SKILL 8   ENDURANCE 14

If you win the fight you may keep the jailer's Dagger (mark it on your *Action Chart* as a Weapon).

If you wish to take the jailer's Keys and free the other prisoners on this level, turn to **125**.

If you wish to head in the direction that the jailer came from, turn to **338**.

If you wish to head in the opposite direction, turn to **333**.

244

As you near the forest, Tanith gives a startled cry. 'Look!' she shouts, pointing behind her. 'They come, the Shadakine come.'

In the distance, you see a chariot hurtling across the bridge.

If you wish to stand and fight, turn to **167**.

If you wish to make a dash for the forest, turn to **13**.

245

'Here,' she says, 'they are both yours if you promise to take me with you. I know the secret ways out of here. I will lead you.'

'Grey Star,' says Shan, 'be on your guard. This witch is a Shadakine slave. How can we trust her?' The Shadakine guards are drawing near.

'We have no choice,' you reply; 'we have to trust her.'

You agree to Tanith's bargain and she hands over your Staff and Backpack. 'Follow me,' she says, opening a door to her right. You both rush through and she closes it behind you, dropping a bar across it to delay your pursuers. You are in a small, sparsely furnished chamber.

'The citadel is honeycombed with secret passages that wind into the hill it stands upon. We will take one of these routes,' she says confidently. She walks to the centre of the room and takes hold of an iron ring that is attached to a flagstone. She pulls on the ring, lifting the flagstone away to reveal a dark passage below. She takes a torch from the wall and enters the passage. 'Come now, they will soon be on our heels.'

You follow without hesitation.

Turn to **292**.

246

The soldier Mantiz springs into action, rushing forward to meet your charge. It is a swift and deadly opponent, and you will need all your skill to break through the dizzying slash and thrust of its large forelegs and nipping pincers. You cannot evade and must fight the soldier Mantiz to the death.

Soldier Mantiz: COMBAT SKILL 14   ENDURANCE 10

If you win the combat, turn to **290**.

247

A piercing cry wakes you with a start. The sickly, old Shianti priest is sitting bolt upright in bed, silhouetted by the pale rays of the moon that shine through the high window of your cell.

'A vision, a vision,' he cries, 'sent from my masters.' He turns and points a gnarled finger towards you. 'You . . .' he shouts, 'you must be helped . . . Come closer, young one.' He rises to his feet, stumbles towards you and whispers in your ear. 'I would repay your kindness,' he says, leaning forward. 'No doubt, you and your friend wish to escape from this terrible place?' he asks. Quickly you nod your assent, pressing the old man to continue 'In my time here, I have learned the safest route of escape. Other prisoners have told me of it.' His strained, bloodshot eyes pierce yours with a mad ferocity. 'I know no way of passing through the door of this cell, but the way beyond the dungeon door is—'

Suddenly he gives a great sigh and falls to the floor. With tears in your eyes, you turn to Shan, who looks anxiously at you. 'He is dead,' you say, sorrowfully. The merchant hangs his head. 'Then we are doomed,' he groans.

Turn to **62**.

248

You slash the tip of your Wizard's Staff across the tendril that is wrapped around your ankle. At the cost of 1 WILLPOWER point, you burn through the tough vine and free your foot. You clamber to your feet only to see the tendrils of another Yaku plant snaking towards you.

With a frightened yell Shan falls to the ground; a Yaku tendril is coiled around both his legs. He hacks at it desperately with his sword.

> If you wish to free Shan by attacking the tendril that drags him towards the waving spines of the Yaku, turn to **204**.
>
> If you wish to strike at the heart of the Yaku plant that attacked you, turn to **229**.
>
> If you wish to loose a bolt of energy at the centre of the Yaku plant attacking Shan (at long range), turn to **254**.

Dodging around the limestone pillars, you enter a sloping defile. It is very steep, and requires considerable effort, reducing your climb to a crawl.

Finally, you reach the top, and pause for breath. The narrow pass opens on to an open plain of sun-baked rock and cracked stones, broken only by sparse lines of gulleys and ravines.

You turn and look back along the pass. Shan has fallen far behind, having covered less than half the distance up the slope. To your horror and amazement you see a creature enter the far end of the defile. It is the wounded Quoku, its body caked with black blood. The creature refuses to die! It creeps along painfully, drawing inexorably nearer to Shan, who seems unaware of the danger below.

> If you wish to shout a warning to Shan, turn to **282**.
>
> If you would prefer to hurry to his side, turn to **257**.

250

Since the corpse of the Shianti priest is still in the dungeon with you, you decide to summon his departed spirit and ask for its aid. With a wedge of rock, you scratch out a ragged pentacle in the dirt of the dungeon floor. Taking a deep breath, you slowly and carefully fall into a trance state. You focus on the body of the dead priest, sending out an echoing call to the spiritual plane. Your mind fills with the groaning cries of disembodied spirits and visions of phantoms with strange pale faces.

Shan the merchant backs away in terror as the trans-lucent Shade of the old priest materializes above its discarded, earthly body, shimmering with a silvery light that illuminates the darkness of the cell. 'I have come, Grey Star,' the Shade says in a hollow voice. 'My aid I give thee, but you must pay the price of the dead if I am to free you. Wilt thou pay this price?'

Your heart is full of fear as you realize that you must agree to the dead man's price without knowing what it will be.

If you wish to accept the dead priest's bargain, turn to **326**.

If you feel that you must refuse, turn to **305**.

251

Just as the two soldiers break through the wall of injured and fleeing people, the illusion takes effect.

'Let me down. Let me down!' an old woman croaks angrily. The approaching warriors and those who carry you on their shoulders stare at you in disbelief. You have transformed yourself into an old woman carrying a walking stick, or at least, that is what the others see.

'Torment a poor old woman would you?' you screech, thumping those nearby on the back, slapping a few heads and tweaking an ear or two before prodding a Shadakine warrior with your Staff. 'And as for you,' you cry indignantly, 'have you no shame? Order this rabble to let me down and show some respect for a woman of my years.' With this, you begin another shower of slaps and thumps to the great amusement of the Shadakine.

Slowly, you are lowered to the ground. Grumbling, you hobble away while puzzled and suspicious eyes look on. However, the Shadakine Warriors are completely fooled, slapping their thighs and roaring with laughter as the stunned crowd disperses in angry silence. A sense of unrest emanates from those who remain behind, and you know that you must leave the harbour area quickly, before your illusion is challenged. An illusion is easily dispelled by one who disbelieves in the image or picture that Enchantment places in the mind, and a visual illusion is hard to maintain for long periods, as details tend to fade and waver after a time, losing their consistency and revealing flaws to the cynical observer.

If you want to leave by the main entrance to the harbour, turn to **50**.

If you would prefer to turn into a dark, narrow street, leading from the harbour area, turn to **40**.

252

You enter the shack and see dust-laden furniture and

a clutter of spades, picks and sieves stacked in one corner. Suddenly a yellow-spotted lizard scuttles out from under the table and dashes towards you.

'It's all right,' says Shan. 'It's a Jerbokan – they're harmless.' The frightened lizard scampers past you and out through the door.

Shan begins to rummage around while telling you that the former occupants were probably jade prospectors, since the Azan River is said to carry deposits of jade, the precious stone used to make Noble pieces. He finds some appetising smoked meat and shares it equally, offering you enough food for 5 Meals. (Remember to mark these on your *Action Chart*.) A further search reveals nothing else of value and you leave the shack.

Turn to **327**.

253

You have climbed only half-way up the steps when the door at the top is thrown open by a Shadakine guard. He regards you with shocked surprise.

If you wish to turn and run back down the stairs and head for the other stairway, turn to **80**.

If you wish to attack the Shadakine guard, turn to **324**.

254

With your eye you trace the tendril that holds Shan back to the main stem. Taking careful aim, you fire at the heart of the plant, destroying it easily at the cost of 2 WILLPOWER points. Immediately Shan is released and he scrambles over to your side as two more creepers wind themselves around your legs. The creepers belong to different Yaku plants and you feel yourself being pulled in two directions at once. Again you drop to the ground and howl in agony as the two Yaku plants attempt to wrench your body apart.

Turn to **279**.

255

The speeding chariot swerves into a skid, and turns over on to its side, throwing the two Shadakine warriors from the vehicle as it flips over. Unfortunately, they are both unharmed and they jump quickly to their feet and charge towards you, scimitars drawn. It is too late to avoid the attack and in order to protect your unarmed companions, you must fight the Shadakine to the death!

2 Shadakine warriors:
COMBAT SKILL 15   ENDURANCE 25

If you win the combat, turn to **75**.

256

The Quoku keep their distance, circling above your heads in lazy spirals. You crouch behind the cover of the large, overhanging rock, trying to guess their next move. 'Why don't they attack?' asks Shan. 'You must have given them a scare. Perhaps they've given up?'

'They're surprised, not scared,' you reply. 'They're planning their next move. While we're holed up in these rocks they lose the advantage of attacking from the air, we're too enclosed for them.'

Daylight has almost faded when the Quoku fly in a

line towards you, each one coming as close as it dares before turning away. Soon they are swooping so close, that you find it hard to resist the urge to duck.

A large rock crashes to the ground by your feet, followed by another. 'They've been ranging-in on us,' you say; 'judging the distance before hurling rocks at us.' Another rock thuds to the ground, dangerously close.

'Their aim is improving,' Shan remarks.

You cannot remain where you are any longer: you are sitting targets. You resolve to make a break for it, and begin to judge the frequency of the stone-throwing Quoku. 'Now – run!' you shout to Shan.

You burst out into the open to a cacophony of Quoku cries. In seconds you realize your mistake: you have played into their hands. Poised on top of the over-hanging rock is the largest Quoku you have ever seen. The huge monster rears up, its yellow eyes glaring with hatred, the poison glistening upon the warts of its slime-encrusted flesh. It leaps and swoops down on you.

If you wish to stand and fight the Quoku, as it hurtles upon you, turn to **281**.

If you prefer to keep running, turn to **306**.

257

You drop back down the slope, half running, half sliding on the gravel of the gully. With Shan at your back, you confront the unyielding Quoku once more.

Using the advantage of standing on the higher ground, you deal the Quoku a crushing blow, sending it tumbling down the slope in a landslide of loose stones and dust. It finally comes to rest in the scree. Your attack has cost you 1 WILLPOWER point.

Turn to **174**.

258

Your sad and troubled mind is further disturbed by the death of the priest, and your sleep is plagued with nightmares of torture and persecution.

Turn to **62**.

259

Inexplicably, the brooding fear that lurks within you is rising uncontrollably. Shan is shaking, his face panic-stricken. Gingerly, you step through the soft mud of the quagmire. The air smells pungently sweet, a cloying odour that is hard to identify. You cannot escape the feeling that there is someone or something else in the cavern, but it is difficult to see in the eerie darkness. The sucking ooze pulls at your feet and in the distance you see a faint light from another passage on the far side of the cavern.

'Grey Star!' shrieks Shan, looking down, his eyes wide with terror. For the muddy cavern floor is comprised of hundreds upon hundreds of corpses, piled high upon each other to form a ghastly mire. Shan is screaming hysterically, but before you can calm him the aura and spirit of this awful place overwhelms your mind, filling it with nightmarish visions.

You are in the Darkling Room of Mother Magri and you must combat its fear if you are ever to leave. Add together your WILLPOWER and ENDURANCE points and use this total as your mental COMBAT SKILL, to be pitted against the COMBAT SKILL of the Darkling Room.

Darkling Room: COMBAT SKILL 28   ENDURANCE 30

If you win the combat, turn to **296**.

260

You turn away and set a swift pace along the tunnel. The soldier Mantiz gives chase and you break into a run. The fearful creature is gaining on you when suddenly you see another of its kind coming from the opposite direction, its long feelers and claws reaching out in anticipation. You are trapped between them and must fight them both together.

2 Soldier Mantiz:
COMBAT SKILL 18   ENDURANCE 20

If you win the combat, turn to **213**.

261

You wake and raise your body slowly. Your head is pounding and your vision is blurred. Realization of your terrible plight comes flooding back and you look around you. In the corner sits a hunched and groaning figure, dressed in furs and gaudy robes now stained with dirt. He sits with his hands clasped over his pot belly. 'Welcome,' he says, sardonically.

You talk to the little man and he tells you about himself. His name is Shan Li, a trader familiar with all parts of the Shadakine Empire and many strange lands beyond. He is a harmless merchant, arrested a few hours ago while in the middle of a drunken reverie in an establishment called the Inn of the Laughing Moon, a popular watering hole for travellers and strangers to the Port of Suhn.

Turn to **291**.

262

The blade misses its target. Slowly you are dragged into a clutch of crimson needles. As the barbs sink into your flesh, your body stiffens with paralysis, relaxing only when death comes mercifully to claim you.

Your life and your adventure end here.

263

Your leg is numb and hinders your climb, but somehow you reach the top of the shaft without falling. You feel the brush of an insect's feeler across your leg and you shudder. A surge of adrenalin rushes through your veins and you clear the last few feet of the shaft with a tremendous physical effort.

You have made it to the surface at last, and blinking in the sunlight, you view a large clearing, surrounded by towering trees and dense, green foliage.

Turn to **146**.

264

Suddenly you remember the Medallion given to you by the 'Redeemer' in the Inn of the Laughing Moon. You take it out and stare intently at the rune inscribed upon it. Surely there is some clue here. You take out the pink potion that the 'Redeemer' gave you and

265

pull out the stopper of the vial. Sniffing the contents
you recognize the scent of Calacena: a mushroom
whose spores induce visions much prized by
magicians and illusionists. With some trepidation you
swallow the potion and discard the contaminated
vial. (Delete this Special Item from your *Action
Chart*.) You stare once again at the Medallion as the
potion begins to take effect.

A close examination of the rune inscribed upon the
Medallion will tell you which section number to
turn to next.

If you cannot solve the riddle of the rune and wish
to take Shan's advice, turn to **190**.
If you cannot solve the riddle of the rune and wish
to seek the counsel of Jnana the Wise, turn to
134.

265

Your Staff erupts into fiery power and you aim a blast
at the Shadakine warriors, injuring the sword arm of

one at the cost of 1 WILLPOWER point. You must fight
the remaining Shadakine to the death.

Shadakine Warrior:
COMBAT SKILL 14   ENDURANCE 18

If you win the combat, turn to **40**.

266 – *Illustration XV (overleaf)*
The evening is full of the sound of the throaty Quoku
call. You both put on a burst of speed, glancing over
your shoulder at your pursuers. To your horror, you
see that they are no longer on the ground! Instead,
they are gliding up into the air, limbs thrust out to
reveal large flaps of membrane that stretch from their
forelegs to their back legs to form gigantic wings. 'You
didn't tell me they could fly!' you shout to Shan.

'I didn't know they even existed until an hour ago,' he
apologizes, wheezing, already short of breath. 'We'll
never outrun them now.'

More Quoku are leaping from their towers of stone,
pushing high into the air with their powerful back legs
and then gliding in circles around their columns,
drifting with the warm air currents. The first of the
creatures climbs gently, rolls to one side and then
pulls into a steep dive. The Quoku hurtles towards
you with astonishing speed; a hawk in pursuit of its
prey.

If you wish to try to evade the diving Quoku, turn to
333.
If you wish to stand and fight, turn to **231**.

XV.   The Quoku hurtles towards you with astonishing speed

267

Panting heavily you sprint up the steep slope of the tunnel. You glance over your shoulder to see many soldier Mantiz scurrying towards you. The tunnel opens into a circular chamber. Leading from the chamber are three exits: two stone corridors, one leading east and one other west, and a narrow tunnel made of earth leading south. You can hear the clack of the insect horde's pincers echoing along the tunnel. You dare not hesitate now.

If you wish to leave the circular chamber by the east corridor, turn to **332**.

If you wish to take the western exit, turn to **340**.

If you would prefer to take the southern exit, turn to **347**.

268

Clambering inexpertly upwards from the base of the cliff, you reach the small cave. You are exhausted. Your thoughts are becoming confused and it is difficult to think clearly. The stagnant odour of the mist above Lake Shenwu fills your eyes and mouth, and your senses rail against it. Inexplicably, you lose another ENDURANCE point and you feel your body weaken.

You pull your head above the lip of the cave and peer in. The interior of the tiny cave is rough-hewn and very small.

If you wish to crawl into the cave and explore its interior, turn to **8**.

If you wish to continue to scale the towering cliff, turn to **113**.

269

Sudden as a whiplash, the Quoku opens its mouth to reveal a long, hollow tongue, curled like a proboscis, which lashes at Shan, coiling around his waist and dragging him towards the amphibian monster.

Shan clings to the end of the Rope for all he is worth.

You pull as Shan's ghastly shrieks echo throughout the gorge, but the Quoku is stronger than you and the Rope is dragged from your friction-burnt hands. (Delete this item from your *Action Chart*).

Turn to **294**.

270

You know that there is no time to lose. Though you do not have your Wizard's Staff, you must make your escape. Hastily, you finish your bowl of rice containing the powdered petals (restore 1 WILLPOWER point and 3 ENDURANCE points) and try to conceive a plan that will secure your freedom.

If you wish to try to sleep now in order to build up your strength, turn to **201**.

If not, turn to **144**.

271

You decide to look for aid on the elemental plane. You drift into a trance and begin to chant, meditating on your need and hoping that the elemental spirits will understand the nature of your predicament. The chant over, you wait. At first, all is quiet and you fear that you have failed. Then a rumbling noise echoes below your feet, and a shuddering tremor makes you stumble.

'Stand by the wall, away from the centre of the cell,' you warn Shan. A large crack appears in the ground, widening to a great hole as the head and shoulders of an Earth Giant smash through the floor. You view the gnarled features of the elemental and his rough, mottled skin of clay with fear and apprehension. Earth Giants are the most stupid of elementals and you doubt if this one will be able to understand fully your needs.

'Escape?' says the Earth Giant, in a stony voice.

'Yes . . . escape,' you say eagerly.

'Tunnel. Wizard follow . . . earth is safe . . . no danger . . . come.' The vast head disappears, leaving a great chasm in the ground.

'Quickly Shan, follow me,' you say, jumping into the open ground. Shan jumps into the darkness behind you and you follow the Earth Giant as it burrows a tunnel, pushing with its great shoulders and clawing at the dirt.

Turn to **273**.

272

You run pell mell along the tunnel, stopping abruptly at the end. For you have made a terrible mistake. The tunnel opens into a vast chamber full of thousands of worker Cave Mantiz and an even greater number of Mantiz larvae.

Enraged at you intrusion, the worker Mantiz surge towards you. You turn back and run as fast as your legs will carry you. Jets of acid burn your arms and legs and you cry out in pain (lose 2 ENDURANCE points).

But there is worse to come. Blocking the exit of the tunnel are two soldier Mantiz. You must force your way past these insects if there is to be any hope of escaping the furious horde.

2 Soldier Mantiz: COMBAT SKILL 20 ENDURANCE 15

If you win the combat in three rounds or less, turn to **322**.

If the combat lasts longer than three rounds, turn to **315**.

273

Suddenly the Giant bursts into a vast cavern, dark with filthy, black mud. 'Man make tunnel here . . . you go up . . . me go down now . . . goodbye.'

With these words, the Earth Giant descends into the ground, the floor rippling to cover his descent as he burrows out of sight. The use of this Magical Power has cost you 1 WILLPOWER point.

You and Shan stand alone in the gloomy cavern, a vague feeling of disquiet stirring in your heart.

Turn to **259**.

274

With a painful jolt, you slam into the lip of the ravine and grab hold of a jutting rock with just one hand. Your grip is slipping. Frantically you search for a secure handhold.

Turn to **306**.

275

It seems as if you have only just fallen asleep when morning comes. With aching limbs, you rise to see that Tanith and Shan are already up and waiting for you.

Turn to **18**.

276

'*Kleasá Tanith, Mundi Gudro,*' chants Tanith, repeating the words over and over.

Suddenly, the darkness is lifted and you see Tanith throw herself on to the raging fire. The black shadow of the Kleasá flies towards her. As the Kleasá engulfs her burning body, she gives one last agonized cry, 'Grey Star, do not fail!'

The fire erupts and in a blinding flash both Tanith and the Kleasá disappear. All that remains is a splash of smoking embers. You swoon and lapse into unconsciousness where you lie.

Turn to **52**.

277

Ready for action, you throw open the door, but there is no one there. Warily you enter the shack.

Turn to **252**.

278

You close your eyes and search into the future. Your power of Prophecy tells you that the way south, towards the Azanam, is to your left. The use of this Magical Power has cost you 1 WILLPOWER point.

Turn to **184**.

279

With some difficulty, you shear through the vine that pulls at your right leg, using up 1 WILLPOWER point.

Shan leaps to your rescue, hacking wildly at the tendril that holds your left ankle. With three clumsy blows, he cuts through the wriggling creeper.

Turn to **128**.

280

The harbour is full with ships of varying kinds, though there is little sign of life. Mooring the small boat, you step on to the stone quayside and survey the harbour area.

'Psst!' a voice hisses at you from out of the darkness. Startled, you spot the crouching form of a one-eyed Suhnese fisherman. 'Come far have we?' he asks, patronizingly. 'And in such secrecy too! Got something to hide have we? Lurking out there at the edge of the bay till nightfall . . . tsk, tsk, very suspicious.'

In vain, you try to convince the one-eyed Suhnaman that you have nothing to hide. 'Saw your sail a long way off,' he sneers. 'Perhaps you're a smuggler, or on the run, I'll be bound. Come now, young master. You can't fool me. What'll you offer to buy my silence?'

With a helpless shrug, you tell him that you have no money. At first, the fisherman seems very angry, but eventually he offers to buy your boat for 20 Nobles, though you cannot be sure that this will keep him quiet.

> If you have the Magical Power of Prophecy and wish to use it, turn to **53**.
> If you agree to sell your boat, turn to **16**.
> If you would rather not sell your boat and wish to continue into the Port of Suhn, turn to **100**.

281

The Quoku hovers in the air, and then sweeps down in an attempt to poison you with its venomous touch.

The slightest contact with this monster's flesh could spell death for you. You must fight defensively. Deduct 1 point from your COMBAT SKILL for the duration of this combat.

Large Quoku: COMBAT SKILL 15   ENDURANCE 30

> You may only fight one round of combat as the Quoku flies past. If your WILLPOWER score is still more than 10, turn to **331**.
> If it is less than 10, turn to **32**.

282

Urgently you call out to Shan. He looks down, and

seeing the grotesque creature that is stalking him, he redoubles his efforts. With uncharacteristic speed he scrambles up the slope, dislodging clouds of dust and gravel with his scurrying feet. As he comes within reach he clutches at your outstretched hand and you haul him over the edge.

Turn to **148**.

283

The raging storm howls all around. Fine dust lashes at your face, courses through your hair and seeps into your mouth until you can hardly breath. Relentlessly you press on, staggering exhausted against the wind. The choking sand causes you to lose 3 ENDURANCE points. At last the storm subsides and you find yourself on the other side of the Wilderwastes, at the edge of the Azagad Gorge.

Turn to **227**.

284

With panic growing like a twisted knot in your belly, you turn back the way you came. As you reach the end of this tunnel you are confronted by two soldier Mantiz out to find the human invader in their midst. Just as you prepare to attack, two more come running from the other direction. You are heavily outnumbered and there is no escape. You must fight all four insects as one enemy.

If you are carrying a lit Torch, turn to **207**.
If you are not carrying a Torch, you must proceed with the battle now.

4 Soldier Mantiz:
COMBAT SKILL 20   ENDURANCE 25

If you win the combat, turn to **310**.

285

Another bolt pierces the heart of the Yaku plant, releasing Shan and costing you 2 more WILLPOWER points. Terrified, he leaps to his feet and runs towards you, stopping only when he is standing next to you.

Turn to **128**.

286

With sweating hands, you fumble with the large bunch of Keys, trying to find one that matches the shape of the lock.

If you have the power of Psychomancy, turn to **235**.

If you do not have this Magical Power, pick a number from the *Random Number Table*.

If the number you have picked is 0, 2, 4, 6 or 8, turn to **214**.

If it is is 1, 3, 5, 7 or 9, turn to **205**.

287

With reckless audacity spurred on by fear, you jump on to the chitinous abdomen of the Cave Mantiz. Before they can react, you have thrown yourself into the shaft, scratching and scrabbling for a handhold in the smooth sides.

Slowly you pull yourself up. A worker Mantiz sends a jet of acid up the shaft, catching your leg. You almost fall as the shock of pain ravages your flesh, burning your calf. (You must lose 2 ENDURANCE points.)

Turn to **263**.

288

You fling the energy ball at the Kazim Stone. The cost of propelling this thought mass costs an extra 2 WILLPOWER points.

There is a tremendous flash as the two forces clash and the energy envelopes the stone. White light fills the room, momentarily blinding you.

Turn to **320**.

289

'Sit, child,' says the old woman, gesturing to the chair opposite. 'I am Mother Magri, seer of the Kazim Stone, Law Giver to the city of Suhn, Truthsayer of Shadaki in the service of the Wytch-king, Shazarak.' The old crone peers at you with hypnotic eyes. 'Look into the Kazim Stone, boy,' she commands, 'that the truth may be revealed.'

Unable to resist, your eyes are drawn by the power of the Stone as it shines brightly, filling the chamber with a lurid yellow glow. With a gasp of horror, you feel fiery fingers reach into your mind and clutch at your will. Your mind is being read by a potent magical force.

If your current WILLPOWER score is less than 15, turn to **150**.

If it is more than 15, turn to **175**.

290

The soldier Mantiz lies dead at your feet. Stepping lightly over the insect's carcass, you enter the passage that it was guarding. After a few minutes the passage splits into two, one tunnel sloping up, the other sloping down.

If you wish to enter the passage sloping up, turn to **267**.

If you wish to enter the passage sloping down, turn to **272**.

If you wish to go back the way you came, turn to **284**.

291

The only other occupant of the cell is a sick old man, who lies, barely moving, upon a wooden pallet. Your Wizard's Staff and Backpack have been taken from you, but you still possess any Items not carried in the Backpack (for example, your Belt Pouch).

Shan turns towards you. 'Innocent. I am innocent of any crime, save the possession of a loud voice and the consumption of too much ale. It is said that those who enter the Hall of Correction are never seen again. Surely, they will not leave us to rot in this hell-hole. What ever am I to do?'

You talk with the merchant for some time discovering many stories about the Lost Tribe of Lara, of their flight into the Shuri Mountains and the legend of their pilgrimage beyond the Kashima Mountains into the Unknown Valley and the Forest of Fernmost. You find yourself growing to like this little man with his dry humour and ironic quips.

'I'll guide you anywhere you want to go, if you can get us out of here,' he says, half joking. But he can see by the look in your eyes, that you take his offer seriously, and that to you escape is not an impossible dream.

Turn to **178**.

292 – *Illustration XVI*

The dark passage seems interminably long, and the three of you are panting for breath before you reach its end. The winding tunnel opens into a large, natural cavern. You rush through the cave mouth and down the steep slope of a hill, stopping only when you reach the bottom. You gasp for breath, your chest heaving and your limbs aching.

If you have the Amulet of the Shianti priest, turn to **346**.

If you do not possess this Special Item, turn to **199**.

293

You turn your back on the impassable cliffs and make your way to the waterfall. Here, the strange vapours of the lake are most concentrated. You lose 1 ENDURANCE point.

XVI.   The dark passage seems interminably long

If you wish to try to swim across the lake, towards the waterfall to see what lies beyond, turn to **318**.

If you wish to make another circuit of the lake to investigate the cliffs on the other side of Lake Shenwu, turn to **343**.

294

Burdened with grief, you stumble like a blind man trailing Shan's backpack on the ground behind you like a dog on a leash. You stagger into the deepening shadows and welcome the inky darkness of nightfall. You are now friendless and alone in a barren wasteland.

If your current ENDURANCE total is less than 10, turn to **319**.

If it is greater than 10, turn to **344**.

295

No matter how hard you resist, the Stone continues to force its way into your mind. Every muscle in your body is tensed and your nerves are shredded.

'Resistance is futile,' says Mother Magri. Her words spur you on and you redouble your efforts. You lose 2 ENDURANCE points as you struggle and still the Stone drains your will.

Fortunately, it is your body that fails you first, and you slump forwards on to the floor, a beaten shell. But the purpose of your mission is safe, for the moment.

'Such is the fate of all who refuse the truthsay of Mother Magri,' she sneers. 'Guards! Throw this one into the dungeon. It seems the stranger desires to hide something of importance.' She then turns towards you, her sinister voice just penetrating your ravaged mind, 'There are other ways of extracting the truth.'

Turn to **187**.

296

Suddenly, the raging assault of the Darkling Room is silent. You grab Shan, who is kneeling in the mud beside you, and drag him towards the far passage, anxious to leave before the Darkling Room can muster another atttack.

You stumble into a long winding passage and run for all you are worth.

Turn to **41**.

297

Using the straw of the dungeon floor to make a small fire, which Shan lights by striking two stones together, you heat the mixture until the crystals have completely dissolved. You plug the stopper into the vial and shake it vigorously. When you are satisfied that the yellow potion is well mixed, you walk over to the door and sprinkle a little of the contents on the lock. A small cloud of yellow gas forms.

Shan looks on, impressed, as the metal of the lock begins to bubble and melt. You have used only half of the potion and the lock is already eaten away. You may keep the remainder of the potion in your Herb Pouch for future use. (Mark this on your *Action Chart* as Ezeran acid in the appropriate section.) However you have used all your sulphur and saltpetre to make the potion. (Remember to erase these from your

Action Chart, although you may keep the two empty vials, which still count as Items, in your Herb Pouch.)

The remnants of the lock fall away, and you push the door open. You and Shan step quietly into a corridor leading to the left and the right.

If you wish to go right, turn to **23**.
If you wish to go left, turn to **333**.

298

At the cost of 2 WILLPOWER points, you fire into the group of workers, throwing them into confusion. The power of the Staff kills one and injures another, causing it to send a spray of its acid all around, injuring another. Seizing your chance you burst into the centre of the confusion and make a running jump for the shaft above.

As you run you step into a pool of acid that burns through your boot, splashing deadly droplets that sear your flesh (lose 2 ENDURANCE points). Too breathless to cry in pain, you reach out and cling to a shallow handhold in the smooth shaft.

The confusion beneath has bought you the time you need to haul yourself up the shaft, and you climb, with agonizing slowness, to the surface.

Turn to **263**.

299

'So be it, wizard,' says the old hag. Once more she draws the power of your assault, bending it to her will and hurling it back. 'Farewell.'

The force of her attack ignites a wall of pain and white

flame in your mind. The very fabric of your soul is torn apart and you collapse to the ground, an empty shell.

Your life and your quest end here.

300

You raise your arms in a gesture of surrender and are immediately seized and led away. Your Wizard's Staff and Backpack are taken from you and your hands are tied behind your back.

You are frog-marched through the city and taken to a large, black stone citadel, called the Hall of Correction, where despite your pleas of innocence, you are unceremoniously dumped. 'You can tell your story to Mother Magri now, stranger,' growls one of the Shadakine. 'The Test of Truth will sort you out soon enough.'

Roughly, you are pushed up a long flight of stone stairs and into a small, bare ante-chamber. An old woman sits at a wooden table. In front of her is a crystal ball, glowing with a dim, yellow light.

Turn to **289**.

301

Your sleep proves both rewarding and refreshing. You have a strange dream, in which Acarya, High Wizard of the Shianti, appears before you. He raises his hands in blessing and chants gently in the tongue of his people. Briefly, you catch a glimpse of the Temple of Amida and a circle of Shianti wizards standing with their hands raised to the sky.

They have sent the power of their thoughts to aid

you. Their blessing strengthens your WILLPOWER, increasing it by 10 points.

Turn to **247**.

302

Shan casts a sheepish glance at you and nervously enters the shack. After a brief pause he returns with a relieved look on his face. 'It's all right,' he says, 'the place is deserted.'

Turn to **252**.

303

You return to the 'Dragon's Teeth'. Trudging through the hot sun, you lose 2 ENDURANCE points due to dehydration and heat exhaustion.

More by luck than judgement, you come, eventually, to the Great Wall of Azakawa. Evening has begun to fall, and in the dwindling light you survey the great cliffs, stretching from east to west as far as the eye can see.

You increase your pace, wishing to reach the Azanam before nightfall.

Turn to **325**.

304

At the cost of 1 WILLPOWER point, you burn through the vine that clasps your ankle. The force of the tendril pulling at your leg causes you to spin to the right, whipping you towards the ugly spines of the Yaku.

Shan leaps to your rescue, slashing at the tendril that threaten to drag you to your doom.

Turn to **128**.

305

You refuse the Shade's price, for you have heard that the dead are seldom fair.

'Very well,' says the old priest's spirit, 'I cannot free you. I will, however freely give advice, since I now perceive that you are a servant of the Shianti race, as I was. If you can find a way past the door of your cell, turn right into the corridor beyond. When you reach the end of the corridor, take the left stairway, and thereafter always turn left and always ascend until you reach the surface. In this way you will reach the gate to freedom. Take no other route, for there only death awaits. Goodbye Grey Star and accept my blessing.'

The old priest's Shade disappears. The cost of this Magical Power is 2 WILLPOWER points.

Now return to **172**, and select another power to aid your escape (you may not choose Evocation a second time).

306

Suddenly the jutting rock falls away and you plunge into the gaping chasm to your death.

Your life and your quest end here.

307

You charge at the wounded Quoku, raising your Staff and readying yourself to deliver a great scything blow.

The enraged Quoku leaps at you and hurriedly you jump to one side, smashing your Staff down on the creature's back. It drops to the ground, knocked senseless by your mighty blow.

Seizing your chance you sprint away with Shan in tow.

Turn to **249**.

308

Taking a deep breath, you plunge into the seething mass and attempt to confront the Shadakine before more people are hurt. Buffeted and crushed by the confused and frightened Suhnese, rushing in all directions, you fight your way to the heart of the chaos.

Through a gap in the crowd you sight the two soldiers, blindly slashing at the terrified crowd. You are standing directly behind them, but the Shadakine are too close to other members of the crowd for you to risk launching an energy bolt from your Staff. Without hesitation, you charge into the fray, staff whirling above your head. You catch the two warriors completely unawares as you attack them from behind, spurred on by a rousing cheer from the crowd. Owing to the surprise of your attack, add 4 points to your COMBAT SKILL for the duration of this combat, remembering to deduct them again as soon as the fight is over.

The Shadakine swing at you with their deadly, gleaming scimitars. You must fight them as one enemy.

Shadakine Warriors:
COMBAT SKILL 20   ENDURANCE 19

If you win, turn to **127**.

309

The unsuspecting guard looks on in amazement as you charge to attack. Owing to the surprise of your challenge you may add 4 points to your COMBAT SKILL for the first two rounds of combat.

Shadakine Guard:
COMBAT SKILL 12   ENDURANCE 16

You may evade this combat at any time and head for the other flight of stairs by turning to **137**.
If you win the combat, turn to **171**.

310

The dead bodies of the soldier Mantiz lie all around you. There is no time to relish the glory of your victory, for the far end of the tunnel is already filling with many more Mantiz, certainly too many for you to challenge single handed.

You dash in the opposite direction and soon arrive at the point where the tunnel divides in two. There can be no going back this time and you have but seconds to choose which passage to take.

> If you wish to take the passage sloping upwards, turn to **267**.
> If you wish to take the passage sloping downwards, turn to **272**.

311

You are seized roughly by the triumphant Shadakine, who lead you away, grinning maliciously. Your Backpack and Staff are taken from you and your hands are tied. For more than an hour you are marched through the streets of Suhn, coming at last to a large, black stone citadel built on a broad hill overlooking Suhn. This is the Hall of Correction, an instrument of Shadakine law more concerned with punishment than order.

A burly Shadakine guard grabs you by the shoulders pressing on your wound where the crossbow bolt's shaft still protrudes; pain shoots through your body. He drags you through the heavy iron doors and throws you to the floor of a sparse, stony entrance hall. The wound has opened again, and warm blood runs down your arm. 'I'm bleeding,' you say to the brutish Shadakine guard. 'I need a Healer. This quarrel must be removed and the wound dressed.'

The Shadakine guard looks at you contemptuously. 'Wound? . . . Dressed? . . .' He snorts with disgust. 'That's just a scratch. I've had far worse fighting in the Old Wars of the Empire. No "Healers" on the field then. Where's your grit, boy?' He steps towards you and grabs at the bolt shaft.

'NO!' you shout, horrified. But before you can stop him, he has torn the bolt from your shoulder, complete with barbed head. You feel that you must faint with pain.

'Healers . . . dress the wound . . . hmph!' the Shadakine mutters to himself. He produces a flask and pulls out the stopper. 'This'll stop the greenrot,' he says, pouring a clear liquid over the wound in liberal quantities, washing away the blood. The liquid burns like acid but it quickly staunches the bleeding. The Shadakine laughs and thumps you on the back, making you flinch.

The crude battlefield remedy has cost you 1 ENDURANCE point, but the treatment is effective, and the injury heals without complications, although you will have a livid scar on your shoulder for the rest of your life.

You are pushed up a long flight of stone stairs and into a small ante-chamber. An old woman sits at a wooden table, her shrunken flesh lit up by the dim yellow light of the crystal ball before her.

Turn to **289**.

312

You have found the Guard room. Six Shadakine warriors overcome their initial surprise and pounce on you, killing you.

You have failed to escape the Hall of Correction and your quest is over.

313

Reaching out with your senses, you probe the minds of those seated near you. Your power reveals to you that the cloaked character in the corner wishes to help you. Indeed, it seems he is waiting for some sign from you. He is a member of a holy order known as the 'Redeemers', pilgrims devoted to a life of silent prayer and the study of the healing arts.

The use of this Magical Power has cost you 1 WILLPOWER point.

Turn to **209**.

314

You hurl the ball of energy into the Kazim Stone at the cost of another WILLPOWER point. Immediately, the assault on your mind stops. The glow of the Stone erupts into a blinding, white light as your ball of power penetrates it. Mother Magri raises her eyebrows and shrugs confidently. She pulls the charged mass of energy towards her and throws your ball of energy back, only now it is greater in strength. As it envelopes you, you lose *half* your current ENDURANCE points total.

If you wish to use 2 WILLPOWER points to duplicate her attack, turn to **320**.

If you do not want to do this, you must use
    2 WILLPOWER points to extinguish the deadly
    circle of light that engulfs you. Turn to **226**.
If you do not have sufficient WILLPOWER points for
    either of these options, turn to **150**.

315

Bravely, you wreak a trail of destruction with your
whirling Staff. But it is already too late. The swarm of
worker Mantiz behind have reached you. You are
dragged to the ground and, screaming in agony, you
are torn into a thousand pieces.

Your life and your quest come to a terrible end here.

316

You slip and fall into the waters below. As you hit the
water you try to scream for the water is burning your
flesh. Water pours into your open mouth; there is no

hope of escape, you sink, unconscious, to the bottom. You have been poisoned by Lake Shenwu.

Your life and your quest end here.

317

You expend a great amount of energy in attempting to move the heavy body of the dead Quoku. Within seconds, you fall paralysed to the ground: the poison that covers the Quoku's warty skin is lethal. You will never know if Shan survived or not.

Your life and your quest end here.

318

You plunge into the waters of Lake Shenwu. You begin to swim when suddenly you feel as if your flesh is on fire. Your body weakens and you start to sink. The waters of Lake Shenwu are poisonous, and even its vapour can kill in a matter of hours. Within a few seconds you have drowned.

Your life and mission end here.

319

Half dazed with fatigue, you stumble in the darkness and fall headlong down a slope of loose shale, finally coming to rest at the bottom. (You lose 1 ENDURANCE point in your fall.)

You are in a wide, shallow basin, on the banks of Lake Shenwu, and you peer around, straining your eyes to see in the darkness of the night.

Turn to **43**.

320

To the amazement of Mother Magri, the light of the Kazim Stone is suddenly snuffed out. You slump forward, exhaused by your exertions, and Mother Magri jumps to her feet, howling curses and abuse.

'You dare to resist!' she screams. 'Guards! Throw this one into the dungeons. It seems that sterner measures are needed to wring the truth from our fledgling wizard,' and she smiles wickedly.

You have exerted 4 more WILLPOWER points and 4 more ENDURANCE points in this duel with the Kazim Stone.

Now turn to **187**.

321

You have entered the jailer's private chamber. He turns and sees you, letting out a startled cry. He draws a small Dagger and charges at you.

Jailer: COMBAT SKILL 8   ENDURANCE 10

You may evade this combat at any time and head for the other flight of stairs, by turning to **137**.
If you win the combat, turn to **37**.

322

You cleave a chaotic path of destruction, clearing the way ahead with only seconds to spare. The swarm of raging worker Mantiz are snapping at your heels and gouts of acid burn into the tunnel walls.

You hurry through the exit of the tunnel and turn the

323

corner to run into another passage, the worker Mantiz barely a few feet behind.

Turn to **267**.

323

You throw the ball of energy at the Kazim Stone, at the cost of another WILLPOWER point. The Stone flares, turning an angry red as the attack hits home. The energy field of your attack lingers and then, to your surprise is absorbed by the Stone, which glows even brighter.

'So it's a fight you want is it?' Mother Magri snarls. She flings the ball of power back at you, now doubled in strength, and as it envelopes you, you lose *half* your current ENDURANCE points.

If you wish to use 2 WILLPOWER points to turn the attack against her, turn to **299**.

If you do not wish to do this you must use 1 WILLPOWER point to extinguish the energy field that surrounds you (or you will lose further ENDURANCE points). Turn to **226**.

324

Too late you realize that he is standing in the doorway of the Guard room. A group of Shadakine warriors pour out of the doorway and bear down on you from above, mercilessly hacking you to pieces.

Your life and your quest end here.

325

The lime stone towers with their tall, ragged peaks, cast lengthening shadows across the broken floor of the gorge. Silhouetted in the orange glow of the evening sun, they unnerve you with their brooding silence.

A strange creaking sound echoes above the muted rush of the Shenwu Falls. It sounds like an old rusty door being opened very slowly. It must be the noise of an animal, although it is quite unlike the cry of any beast that you have ever known. You hear the sound again, over to your right and then again, ahead of you, as if in answer.

A sense of grave danger washes over you, and Shan, infected by your disquiet, has paled with fear. With slow, careful steps, you move forwards. The hairs on the back of your neck prickle, and you have the distinct feeling that many eyes are watching you.

Turn to **136**.

326

Warily, you agree to accept the dead priest's offer.

'So be it,' drones the Shade. 'For my part, I will give you the help you seek, since I now perceive that you are a servant of the great Shianti race, as once was I. You must turn right beyond the door of this cell and, when you reach the end of the corridor, take the left stairway. Thereafter always turn left and always ascend, until you reach the surface. In this way you will come to the inner courtyard where the gate to freedom stands. Take no other route, for death awaits you any other way.'

'What then is the price I must pay?' you ask.

'You must free the dead of this place. Step outside the pentacle and speak the forbidden tome that will release the wronged souls that have died here. The dead desire their revenge on those who cruelly murdered them. Deny them not, for your soul will be forfeit if you do.'

You are filled with dread. It is forbidden by Shianti law to free the dead upon the Earth, for once freed by the 'forbidden tome', they can never be controlled. They will roam the Earth eternally, able to act in any way they choose, whether for good or ill.

If you agree to speak the tome, turn to **87**.
If you deny the dead, turn to **220**.

327

You head south across the desolate plain but after a few minutes Shan stops, shielding his eyes with his hand as he peers eastwards. 'Can you feel it?' he asks.

At first you are not sure what he means, but then you notice that the atmosphere has changed. A wind has started up, and tumbleweeds and pools of fine brown dust eddy in busy spirals. Shan points towards the horizon and you spot a great cloud of dust rolling towards you.

'Dust storm,' says Shan. 'Looks like a mean one.'

If you wish to head back to the shack and take cover, turn to **78**.

If you would rather keep moving on towards the Azanam, turn to **283**.

328

You hit the line of the river and pick your way south. Owing to your long exposure to the scorching sun you must lose 2 ENDURANCE points. When at last you come to the point where the Yaku plants grow, you resolve to stay with the river and overcome the difficulties of the dense undergrowth, as best you can.

Turn to **104**.

329

Your Staff burns a great hole in the nearest Yaku plant, killing it instantly at the cost of 1 WILLPOWER point. Unfortunately, it was not an attacker, and still the two Yaku plants pull at you with an ever-tightening grip. You grit your teeth against the pain. Your right leg is being wrenched from your body and you must lose 4 ENDURANCE points.

Turn to **42**.

330

As the Quoku dives towards you, you suddenly change direction, sprinting towards an overhanging rock face that will shield you from attack. As you dive into the hollow space beneath the overhang, you turn to see the creature screech with horror as the low curve of its high speed dive brings it on a collision course with the ceilinged wall behind. It flaps its wings desperately, climbing at an acute angle and only just gaining enough height to clear the wall. Shan gives a shout of delight. 'Quick thinking,' he says, laughing through his fear. 'Maybe these bird-brained frogs are a bit stupid, eh?'

You smile and give him a reassuring nod. Privately, you are not so sure that they are.

Turn to **256**.

331

A deft blow with your Staff wounds the Quoku, making a long slash across its soft underbelly, which you can see as it flies over your head. The Quoku clutches at its wound and tumbles to the ground. But it quickly recovers and launches itself once again into attack, crying with the fury of an animal in pain.

If you wish to fight the Quoku, turn to **307**.
If you would prefer to evade combat, turn to **182**.

332

With fear surging through every nerve, you dart into the east tunnel. The insect horde sweeps towards you and a soldier Mantiz, faster than the others, reaches out and claws at your leg, raking a crimson weal of pain along your calf. With a howl of agony, you stumble, and half diving, half falling, roll along the ground, twisting to face the creature as it rears up before its prey.

If you have your Wizard's Staff, turn to **96**.
If you do not, turn to **9**.

333

You are walking along a steeply sloping passage that grows darker as it heads deeper. It is almost pitch black when you come to a vast open cavern. With fear in your heart, you step into the cavern, your feet squelching on the filthy, black mud that is the floor.

Turn to **259**.

334

You reach the end of the sloping passage. It opens into a larger tunnel that divides and curves away to the left and right. As you look around, you realize where you are.

You have entered a Cave Mantiz nest. The Cave Mantiz live in colonies below ground in much the same way as their smaller cousins, the ants. They burrow their nests out of hard stone, dissolving the rock with a potent acid stored in their bodies. If you can find your way through the maze of the nest, you should be able to reach the surface above the Wall of Azakawa and enter the Azanam.

If you wish to take the left passage, turn to **222**.
If you wish to take the right passage, turn to **234**.

335

You realize that there is no hope of Shan's survival. You have lost a valued friend and now you must continue your journey alone. You pick your weary way around the ravine and press on towards the Shenwu Falls.

Turn to **294**.

336

The Suhnese are rushing in all directions as the Shadakine rain sword blows on anyone unfortunate enough to be standing too close. Quickly you survey the scene. You note that there are two exits from the harbour area: one is the main entrance, but this is blocked by the cruel Shadakine who seek to control the riot; the other is a narrow street.

If you wish to leave the harbour by the narrow street, turn to **40**.
If you wish to leave the harbour through the main entrance, turn to **50**.

337

You leap into attack, causing the Quoku to release the unconscious Shan.

Wounded Quoku:
COMBAT SKILL 14   ENDURANCE 18

If you win the combat, turn to **44**.

338

You head down the corridor with Shan following close behind. Two stairways lead from the corridor and you must choose which to take.

If you have the power of Prophecy and wish to use it, turn to **92**. (Note down this section number as you will need to return to it later.)

If you wish to take the left stairway, turn to **137**.

If you wish to take the right stairway, turn to **212**.

339

As you approach the bar, the innkeeper booms out in a loud voice. 'Greetings, young stranger. What is your pleasure?'

You order a mug of ale, which costs 1 Noble. (Remember to mark this from your *Action Chart*.)

> If you wish to begin a conversation with the innkeeper, turn to **217**.
> If you do not, turn to **105**.

340

Running west along the empty corridor, you notice that the tunnel begins to slope upwards. As it narrows, you see a group of worker Mantiz ahead intent on some task. Sunlight streams down through a shaft above their heads. You see that they are boring into the rock in front of them and suddenly you realize that this passage is unfinished.

A swarm of crawling soldier Mantiz lies behind you, their pace and numbers increasing; you are trapped between them and the wall of the unfinished tunnel. Your only hope is the vertical shaft above the burrowing workers, for you are sure that the surface lies beyond. But first, you must pass the workers.

> If you wish to attack them with your Wizard's Staff before they have had a chance to see you, turn to **298**.
> If you wish to try to jump on to the back of a Cave Mantiz standing directly below the opening of the shaft, turn to **287**.

341

Without once missing your footing, you reach the other side of the Azan River. You head towards the cliffs but your reactions are slow and you are becoming increasingly uncoordinated. You slip and fall to the ground. (Lose 1 ENDURANCE point.)

By the yellow light of the mists of Lake Shenwu, you survey the cliffs once more. The cliffs on this side of the lake are jagged and pitted with myriad cracks and crags.

You decide to try to climb the cliffs at this point. With groping hands, you reach for the small crevices and crannies of the cliff face. After climbing for a while you see a small cavern directly above your head. Kicking with your feet, you scramble in.

Turn to **8**.

342

With an immense effort of will, you haul yourself up and over the edge of the precipice, scraping your body over the razor sharp rocks and tearing the flesh of your hands and arms, leaving bloody weals of pain. Blood courses freely down your limbs from these wounds and you must lose 3 ENDURANCE points.

Turn to **74**.

343

You walk along the banks of Lake Shenwu. The easiest point to cross is where the Azan River starts, for Lake Shenwu is its source. The waters here still glint a dirty yellow colour, although the luminous mist is less dense. You lose 1 ENDURANCE point as a sleepy feeling begins to overtake you.

If you wish to try to wade across the River Azan, turn to **17**.

If you would rather try to jump across the stepping stones, turn to **242**.

344 – *Illustration XVII*

Soon, you come to a wide basin below the Shenwu Falls and the Great Wall of Azakawa. You are standing by the banks of Lake Shenwu, and in the eerie darkness it is a strange and disturbing sight.

Turn to **43**.

345

You concentrate, trying to visualize the threat before it happens. But you receive no vision from the future and conclude that whatever is menacing you must be something unknown to your experience. Instead, your mind rings with the warning: 'Death from above.' The use of this Magical Power has cost you 1 WILLPOWER point.

Turn to **61**.

346

As you and your companions stop to catch your breath, you turn and look behind. The citadel looms high above you, its bleak stone walls crumbling to the ground. It is enveloped by a strange mist and the shadowy forms of the dead dance around it. Stone by stone they raze the prison to the ground. The shrieks and howls of the Shadakine echo beneath the starlit sky as they meet a grisly death at the hands of their past victims.

XVII.   You come to a wide basin below the Shenwu Falls
and the Great Wall of Azakawa

347

'Was it you who called the dead?' asks Tanith, her eyes wide. You nod, a chill running down the length of your spine.

'A horrible death,' she remarks coolly. 'Shazarak would have approved.' She seems unaware of the ironic nature of her statement as you hang your head in shame.

Turn to **199**.

347

Head bent low, you hurl yourself into the narrow tunnel. It slopes upwards, becoming narrower as it winds and curls like a snake. Ahead you see a lone worker Mantiz coming towards you, holding a large leaf in its pincers. Without hesitation, you dive over the Cave Mantiz, scraping your back against the walls and ceiling of the converging tunnels. A gout of acid misses your body by inches as you tumble to the ground on the other side of the insect. You roll over twice before leaping to your feet once more.

Countless numbers of snapping, malicious insects pursue you, but far ahead you see a dim light, which fills you with hope. A faint gust of air blows against your cheek, making you certain that this tunnel connects with the surface. You focus on the dim light, and force your aching legs to propel you onwards.

As you grow nearer the flood of light, you see that the tunnel ends at a blank wall. Your spirits sink: are you trapped after all?

Turn to **47**.

348

You pass into a state of shock, a semi-conscious state that blanks your mind, screening it from the Kazim Stone. Mother Magri gives a frustrated cry. You are beyond her grasp, safe in a realm of oblivion.

Turn to **187**.

349

It is Tanith, the girl in the service of Mother Magri. She is carrying your Wizard's Staff and Backpack. 'Grey Star!' she calls. 'I've found you at last.'

'We are trapped!' shouts Shan. At the other end of the passage you can hear the echo of running feet and the rasping voice of Mother Magri ordering her Shadakine warriors to find you.

If you wish to attack the young girl, turn to **173**.
If you wish to try to persuade her to relinquish your Staff and Backpack and let you pass, turn to **245**.

350 – *Illustrations XVIII – XIX (overleaf)*

A great hooting yell signifies the presence of others in the leaf-green light of the tree tops. Some forty ape-like men with long tails swing bundles of smoking leaves at the end of lengths of vine. The smoke gives off a choking stench that throws the huge insects into confusion. Within a few moments, they have dropped from the branches of the tree or are scurrying back along the trunk, fleeing from the swirling fumes.

Through watering eyes, you watch the strange, stunted men using their tails to swing from tree limb to branch with astonishing agility, and flushing out the insect invaders with practised ease. These are the Kundi. You have found the Lost Tribe of Lara.

As you watch the one-sided battle draw to a close, two sets of hairy arms grab you and lift you bodily into the air. Your ape-like abductors carry you through the giddy heights, leaping and swinging from tree to tree, tossing you like a bale of hay. You are being carried through a fine mist of cloud, from which the Azawood tree draws much of its moisture. Up here, in the highest levels of the forest, is a complex of wooden houses and platforms. You are dumped unceremoniously, outside the largest of these tree houses: the house of the Kundi king.

The old king regards you with undisguised displeasure. 'I am Okosa, Kundi king – why you come and who are you?'

Quietly you tell the king of your quest for the Moonstone of the Shianti, your search for the Shadow Gate and your need of the magical Kundi vision to guide you there.

'You no Shianti . . . You bring creeping death from below . . . Kundi guide you nowhere,' he says, eyeing you suspiciously. No matter how you try, you cannot convince him that you are a Shianti wizard and that you were trying to escape from the terrible Mantiz attack, not leading it. He turns his back on you with a derisive snort.

'I can make great magic,' you say hopefully, 'ancient magic, the Way of the Shianti.'

'Wytch-king make magic, Shadakine make magic. This prove nothing,' the king replies with a dismissive wave of the hand.

'How then, can I prove the truth of my words to you?' you ask, helplessly.

The Kundi King gives you a sly look over his shoulder, eyebrows raised. 'Prove?' he says. 'Yes, you prove many things I think, when Urik, wise elder of the Kundi Tribe has words with you. Then you see some *Kundi* magic! Not Shadakine spells and whispers.'

Patiently, you wait. Faintly, you can hear the jingling of tiny bells and a hoarse voice chanting a monotonous rhythm, tunelessly. At length, a wizened old Kundi is led into the room. He is covered in bird feathers and numerous small bells and his mad, bulging eyes roll around their sockets. The Kundi king and the old Kundi's escorts look to him with reverence, for he is their Shaman and a respected figure in their society. To your eyes, however, he looks faintly ridiculous, shambling around you in a comic, bow-legged dance, waving and rattling a strange, fur-

XVIII.   The strange stunted men use their tails to swing
from tree limb to branch with astonishing agility, and flush
out the insect invaders with practised ease

covered talisman in your face and repeating his dissonant litany in an endless monotone. Your own instinctive powers tell you that no magic is being performed here and you look with interest, curious to see what happens next. Suddenly the mad old Kundi falls silent. He is short of breath, his bony chest wheezing. He bares the blackened stumps of his rotten teeth and pressing his face close to yours, so close that you can smell the stink of his fetid breath, he speaks to you.

'You no look like Shianti,' he says, looking you up and down with a theatrical gesture.

'Shianti *wizard*,' you correct, drawing no response.

'You no feel like Shianti,' Urik continues, running his leathery fingertips along the filthy, tattered remains of your robe. He wrinkles his nose. 'You no smell like Shianti . . . smell more like swamp!' he says, exploding into a great fit of hoarse laughter, clapping his hands with glee.

'You see Shianti, you say?' he then asks, his eyes narrowing.

You nod your assent.

'The youngest Kundi child knows the 'riddle of the Shianti'. If you have truly looked upon them, then you will know the answer.'

The fate of your quest hangs upon the words of a child's nursey rhyme it seems. Okosa, the Kundi king agrees to grant you a guide to the Shadow Gate, only if you can answer the old Shaman's rhyme. Anxiously, you listen to his words, burning them into your mind.

XIX. A wizened old Kundi covered in bird feathers and
numerous small bells is led into the room

'Answer me this, wizard . . .

> *Wise Shianti and Kundi man,*
> *Look eye to eye in tree,*
> *Shianti man see Kundi man,*
> *But what does Kundi see?'*

The solution to the rhyme can be found in part two of the Grey Star series

RANDOM NUMBER TABLE

3	2	7	9	6	2	8	2	5	6
4	1	3	8	7	1	6	8	4	0
4	1	6	3	1	7	5	6	2	0
2	5	0	4	8	6	6	8	4	1
0	5	9	5	7	0	9	4	6	5
2	8	2	5	6	3	2	7	9	6
1	6	8	4	0	4	1	3	8	7
7	5	6	2	0	4	1	6	3	1
6	6	8	4	1	2	5	0	4	8
0	9	4	6	5	0	5	9	5	7